Lola

Lola

TANISHA RENEE

Sky's The Limit Publications

PUBLICATIONS

Sky's The Limit Publications
P.O. BOX 10537
Daytona Beach, Florida 32120

First Printing 2018
Cover Design by Miami Kaos
Manufactured in the United States of America
ISBN-13: 978-0-9906235-2-6
ISBN-10: 0-9906235-2-1
10 9 8 7 6 5 4 3 2 1

Dedicated to my inspiration for Nana. Granny- you were an angel on earth who finally got her wings... soar high my love. You will dance and smile forever in my heart.

Thank you to my readers and Secret Sessions book club members who continue to support me! Your messages keep me going! We're back with another one! Peace & blessings to the universe! xoxo

"Maybe I had it all wrong. I'm not mad at you hoes." – Lola

Lola

Crew Love

"The world is yours. Whose world is this?" sang Nas through the speakers, as the trees whizzed by in the humid October night. Lights and exit signs appeared in view as the car merged over to get off exit 92. The car approached the light, the radio was muted. "Now we gon' go in there, rock this nigga. And peel the fuck out n'ahmean?" shouted Rico to his three passengers.

"Hell yea." replied the front seat passenger, Quan. He fired up a Newport, dusting off his pants as he placed gloves over his hands. He passed guns to the backseat riders. Gloves already on, they placed their masks over their faces as the car turned off 436 and onto a side street. They had done this scene, it seemed a million times before. Robbing had become second nature to the crew, willing to go near and far for the lik that would keep them set for a while. This hit had become personal, and had to be dealt with. The car slowed down before coming to a complete stop along the curb. Everyone scanned the scene, looking over the two story brick, dimly lit house, with a fenced yard. Rico reached under the seat for his heat, before exiting the car. "Let's go." Everyone followed his lead exiting the vehicle. The backseat riders jumped the fence heading to the back door, the others to the front. Rico tapped on the door with the barrel of the gun. After waiting a few minutes he heard the shuffle of an angry foot. "Shit! Who the fuck?" said a man.

He heard another set of footsteps going in the opposite direction. Quan looked at Rico; he placed his hand over the peep hole. "Who is it?!" shouted the man angrily. After no answer, he pulled back the curtain of the window beside the door. POW! POW! Went the fire from Rico's gun blasting the man in his face. He fell dead to the floor. Quan shot off the door knob and they proceeded into the house.

"Ahhh!! A woman screamed from the kitchen. The backdoor flung open in came the other two, dressed in all black. She screamed again dropping her glass.

"Don't fucking move!" shouted one of the masked assailants.

"Okay. Okay. Please don't shoot me!" One of the assailants grabbed her by her thick brown hair, leading her towards the living room. The woman began to quiver. Her bare nipples becoming erect and her perfectly waxed vagina exposed, she held her hands in the air as tears fell from her eyes. The woman, mixed, no older than twenty, with a rose tattoo on her thigh and stiletto nails screamed jumpoff. Moments later gunshots went off upstairs, the woman began to shake.

"Shit! One of the assailants screamed heading up the stairs. The woman now with one assailant began to plead for her life.

"Please. Don't kill me? I'll do whatever you want! Money? I know where Gino keeps his money. I'll suck your dick. Whatever you want, please don't kill me!"

There were three more shots and the thud of feet running downstairs. She looked up seeing the other three with multiple bags in their hands. The woman quivered again.

"Please! Tears fell from her eyes again." Damn! That's a sexy bitch!" screamed Quan from his mask. Rico laughed loudly, his infectious laugh could melt any woman. The assailant cleared their throat holding the woman.

"A'ight, A'ight. Do whatever." said Rico as they walked out the door. The others followed, as the assailant hit the woman across the face with the gun. She screamed holding her face.

"And no I don't need you to suck my pussy, bitch!" the woman's mouth dropped hearing a woman's voice behind the mask. The assailant turned to leave with her crew, the woman reached for a statue on the table. She turned around firing two shots at the woman one hitting her in stomach. She screamed in agony.

"Don't try me bitch!" she walked out the door seeing the others in the car. The lights came on from the driveway she pulled out her gun. "Come on Lo." she heard the driver say from the driveway. She looked over at the black BMW in the driveway, seeing Caesar behind the wheel. She smiled running over to the passenger side. As they all sped off into the night.

They immediately hit the highway, heading back home to Jacksonville. Lola took off her mask. Her black tresses fell down her back, her caramel skin, almond shaped chestnut eyes, and full soft pink lips exposed. Caesar looked over at her. "You ended her, didn't you?"

"Nah, But it just amazes me how bitches, just immediately think pussy solves everything!"

"Cuz' it does! Replied Caesar, I would've let that bitch get it."

She rolled her eyes. "Whatever. So how much?" she replied as she rested her arm in the window.

"Shit. About a good seven g's a piece. After we flip some of the other shit they got in there and this Beemer. We'll be looking at a good twelve." "Cool." said Lola as she looked off into the night's sky. Once back at their spot to split up the money, Lola took a cab home. She looked around at the city lights, thinking of how many good summers she had in Duval or was she trippin' again off the "dirty" she had smoked earlier. On the seldom occasions she did smoke a dirty, she always had mixed emotions about her reality. In reality, her summers were fucked up and her insecurities at time had gotten the best of her. Her main goal was to make sure her nana was good and that she was happy. Lauren "Lola" Rose was born in Washington D.C. All she ever knew was that her father was from Trinidad and her mother was Thai. She was left on the doorstep of a local church at age of one, and the woman she had affectionately named her Nana, was the one who found her. Anna Rose was a beautiful woman with a humble spirit. She always wanted to do good for others and the community. She had found Lauren outside with a note attached to her stroller. It was raining and here sat this beautiful baby girl, with a smile on her face. The note said.

Please, take her. She doesn't cause much trouble. Her name is Lauren. Thank you.

Every time Lauren thought of the note it sent an uneasy feeling inside. But Anna had taken the beautiful baby in and in years after no family came forth, adopted her. Nana was an African-American, god fearing woman, from Miami, Florida. After five years, her cousin decided to start a new church in Jacksonville area and asked for help. Anna figured this would be a fresh start for her and Lauren. As a single mother, she had lost her only son David, to a drive by shooting in Miami at the age of seventeen; she wanted no more to do with Miami. She threw herself into church and on her second month being in New Hope Church, is when she found Lauren. She figured it was a sign. Lauren loved Anna. But hated how she never fit in, she felt that everyone knew because of her silky hair and exotic looks that she wasn't truly Anna's. At family events, she was teased by the other kids because of her chinky eyes, and long legs. Anna always told her she was beautiful but she always felt, she wasn't ever good enough. She smiled thinking about Anna as the cab stopped in front of their home. She paid the twenty dollar fare, looking up at their townhome. She closed the car door, placing her mask in her book bag. She opened the gate walking up to her house. "Nana! I'm here!" she placed the keys on the table taking off her hoody placing it on the chair by the door. Wearing a white tee, black joggers and black Timberland boots her size six frame and curves would cause anyone to double look. Her curves, rarely seen under her layers of clothing and she rarely wore her hair down outside. She continued upstairs to Anna's room. "Nana!" she said happily. She walked over to her bed, seeing her frail body. Lola held back her emotion seeing her in this state. Anna looked over to her.

"My Lola, How are you?" she replied clearing her throat. "I'm good. But that's not important, how are you?"

"I'm okay, as long as God is on my side, I'm amazing." she smiled. Lauren loved this about Nana she was always positive. She ran her fingers through Anna's hair. "What about your meds? You got them? Did you take them?" she looked over the dresser seeing her pill boxes were empty. Lauren had been gone for two weeks, out on the low with the crew. "I took a pain pill today. But, I think my other pills are out." Lauren looked at her empty pill bottles. "You're out of everything. Who's been here?" "No one." said Anna. Lauren threw the bottles down disgusted. "I'll get these refilled tomorrow. You eat?" "I couldn't make the steps today, baby." said Anna softly. Lauren looked at her saddened about her not eating she went downstairs and prepared her food.

After feeding and preparing Anna a bath she brushed her hair laying her back in bed. Anna smiled. "I love you, my little Lola." "I love you too." said Lauren kissing her cheek. Lola looked down into her beautiful mother's face as she drifted to sleep. She fluffed the pillows on her queen sized bed before sliding out. Lola placed her phone on her dresser looking over the note which was attached to her mirror, which had been pinned to her stroller. Glancing at her reflection in the mirror, she pulled her hair up looking at her bone structure, trying to give her most seductive face. Not pretty enough. Her hair fell limp as she took off her clothes heading to the shower.

Days later she was getting ready to go with her crew. Anna was feeling better today and was downstairs on the recliner watching television and eating grapes. Lauren set her a plate of spaghetti, her pill box and drink beside her. "Nan, I'll be back." "Okay." she said with a smile. "I refilled your meds; they are in here and if you need me call. If not Ms. Loretta is next door today, she'll come over." "Okay. I'm fine." She heard the horn outside. She smiled. "Love you. Bye." Lauren walked outside seeing Caesar in the passenger seat and Rico behind the wheel of a black Chevy Suburban. She hopped in the back seat. Rico turned around smiling at her. "What up Lola!" he said excitedly. "What's good?" she replied hitting him and Caesar on the shoulder. "Well, tonight we going out and later we have another spot to get. You down?" said Rico. "Of course she's down. You know Lola one of the niggas." shouted Caesar. Lauren looked out the window. "It's gonna be bad bitches at this shit tonight. I'm goin' all in tonight." said Rico. Lauren rolled her eyes.

"Typical fuckin' niggas, it's all about pussy." she said dryly. Rico laughed.

"I mean, when you look as good as me. Bitches all over the kid." Lauren laughed. Rico looked at her through the rearview mirror a smile on his face. She looked back at him. He was attractive, 5"10", brown eyes, long lashes, mahogany skin, muscular build. He always sported a low fade and body was covered in tattoos. He was the loose cannon of the crew at any given time he would pop off. In the streets that fact synonymous with his name. Caesar on the other hand was Puerto Rican, 5"7", always sported fresh waves, goat tee, stayed high and was the joker of the group. He was the fashion forward, *"suave"* nigga of the crew he affectionately called himself. Quan: Bahamian and always wanted to fit in, the quiet one which, Rico always said that means he's plotting. Because Quan had so many different connects on guns and drugs they felt he was pertinent in any of their schemes, although he would never plan any, he was always down. The others knew he was infatuated with Lola and always used it against him when he made gestures, to get her to notice. They arrived at the "dungeon" as they called it, which was their chill spot. Rico came around to the trunk taking out cases of beer, Hennessy and Grey Goose. Lola helped out walking into the house. Quan met them outside. "Sup' Lola. Said Quan a wide smile formed across his lips. "Sup." said Lola nonchalant. Rico and Caesar burst into laughter at Lola's blatant curve. Lola sat down on the couch kicking her Timberlands up on the coffee table. Rico grabbed a red plastic cup filling it with Henny sitting beside Lola. He looked over at her. "You want a drink?" "Hell yea, nigga. You gon' fix it?" "You got two legs. I ain't fuckin' you." Everyone laughed. Lola smirked. "And you never will." said Lola. Rico sat up, pulling a bag of weed from his coat. Lola went to make her drink.

"Yo, I got a hit for us in St. Augustine. Homie driving the fucking transport truck for Benz, said it should have a few other joints on there we can flip that shit." said Caesar as he looked at the others for a response. "I mean that's cool and all, but the only way that shit will work if each of us, take a whip to the shop to be flipped. Feel me?" said Lauren. Rico nodded his head in agreement as he put the finishing touches on the blunt he was rolling. Caesar glanced over at Quan, before smirking at the idea.

"Who got time for that fuck shit? How about we go in and steal whole fucking truck!" Rico smiled at the idea as he fired up the blunt, taking a few hits before passing it over to Lola. "Here he go with this crazy shit! Do you, I'll do me." Quan looked over at Lauren. She laid her head against the couch, looking up at the ceiling.

"I'm saying are y'all down or what? What y'all scared now?" taunted Caesar as he took a sip of Henny from his cup.

"Nah, never that. I'm just saying we need to have shit planned out." said Lauren.

"We're gon' be ready. When have we not been ready?" said Caesar sarcastically. As the blunt continue to be passed around the room, all of them were high. Rico had formulated a plan. The hit was to take place that next Wednesday, at three a.m. Two were to be hidden in two of the cars on the back of the truck. The other two were to follow the truck in their car. They had planned a hit like this before, but didn't think they had the muscle. So Rico planned to kill the driver if things got out of hand and take the whole truck. They all agreed and decided they will meet up Tuesday to iron out any last details. Lauren got up from the couch now feeling the buzz from the Henny. She stumbled as she got to her feet. Rico laughed hitting Lauren on the butt. "You okay Lo? Ain't nobody carrying you home! Everyone laughed. You alright?" Lola's eyes were low and she could barely see what was going on. She squinted her eyes. Caesar burst out in laughter.

"Yo! I've never seen Lola like this! She's fucked up!" Caesar's eyes were low as well, but he just felt a buzz. Lola attempted to walk to the kitchen and the room began to feel as if it were spinning. "Yo… Room is feeling like it's going round and round, right now. Y'all feel that?" said Lola standing still. They all begin laughing again.

"She's lit son." Said Rico.

Lola began to sweat fanning herself. It feels like it's ninety degrees in here! She shouted. Everyone stared at her. She attempted to walk again and she tripped over the table. She fell to her knees. Everyone laughed again. There was a knock at the door Caesar got up to answer it. There stood three women, scantily dressed. What's good Caesar? Said the leader as they entered the house. The leader Puerto Rican, shoulder length curly hair, wearing a pink strapless body con dress that accentuated every curve, barely covering her round bottom. Pink glittered toes in her six inch heels. Caesar smiled as the other two walked in behind her. One black, the other white. The black female was wearing a black netted crop tank and boy shorts made of pleather. Her thick thighs and round backside immediately got the other's attention. She was wearing a long black weave that stopped at her derriere. The white female had long blonde hair, tall, slender with DD breast and bright green eyes. She was wearing a spaghetti strap dress, which was silver and tight. Caesar smiled at her. "What's going on? Is the party started yet?" said the white female.

"Nah, baby. It's just started. What's your name? Said Caesar.

The Puerto Rican female interjected.

"I'm Mimi. Toya. She stated pointing at the black female. Cara. She pointed to her opposite side, to the white female." The men stared at the women. Mimi walked over to the stereo turning it on. Rihanna's voice boomed thru the speakers. She began dancing slowly and seductively. Cara walked over to the bottle of Henny placing the bottle to her lips. Toya soon followed her. The men kept their eyes glued to them. Lola lay on the floor on her back now. The three women began dancing on each other. Grabbing each other's breasts and grinding on one another to the music. Mimi hit Cara on the ass. Cara smiled sweetly grabbing Mimi's chin kissing her on the lips. Rico grabbed his dick. Toya began to bend over making her ass clap to the beat. As all eyes went to Toya, Cara sauntered behind her ass licking her camel toe through her shorts. Cara squatted low, making sure to keep her tongue pursed to Toya's ass. She opened her legs wide showing her perfectly waxed pussy. Caesar bent down so he could see all of her as he grabbed himself as well. Cara held on to Toya's legs and began to lick Toya's pussy again while in between her legs. Toya began to fondle her own breast, while getting lower for easier entrance for Cara.

Mimi smiled walking over to Lola. She bent over her, seeing her eyes closed. She looked at the men for permission. Rico smiled. She proceeded down to the floor, she climbed on top of Lola. Straddling her with her thick thighs. She began to kiss Lola's cheek and ear. Lola remained still. She pulled her shirt over her head and revealed her black cotton bra. Rico sat fully erect. The mystery of seeing his comrade naked, had him watering at the mouth. He always wondered what was under the baggy clothes but she was his nigga, so he never seen her in any other way until now. Toya had laid Cara on top of the coffee table and taken off her dress exposing her perky silicone titties. She gently parted her legs, before placing her head in between her thighs. Mimi had begun kissing Lola's breast through the bra, she worked her way down her washboard abs. Lola's eyes were still closed as Mimi unbuckled her pants. Quan sat up, his dick erect, he didn't know what to do. Should he let Mimi go through with this or stop her? He wanted Lola for himself but it didn't hurt seeing her naked either with a beautiful woman. Mimi placed her fingers in Lola's panties she began fingering her gently. Caressing her own breasts with her other hand. Rico couldn't take anymore. He unzipped his pants exposing his dick. Toya came over to him and began giving him head. Caesar soon followed with Cara, with their own head session Quan was stuck staring at Lola and Mimi.

Lola's mouth parted open as she let out a moan. Mimi smiled as she began rougher. "That's right... speak to me sexy." said Mimi. She pulled off Lola's pants and panties which were black boy cut briefs. Quan couldn't help but glance over at Lola's beautiful pussy, trimmed, fat and pink. Mimi began to devour her lips in her mouth, licking her clit slowly. Lola moaned again. Quan's dick was throbbing through his jeans he wanted Lola now. He began stroking himself. Mimi got off the floor walking towards Caesar. Cara walked over to Quan, she began giving him head as he watched Lola on the floor, imagining her with him right now. In minutes nothing could be heard but the sound of skin clapping and moans.

Four days later and Lola hadn't talked to the crew since she woke up half naked. She didn't know what happened and hated that she had possibly showed vulnerability and let one of them get her open. All she remembered was leaving out the front door and walking home. She wasn't a virgin, but she wasn't about just lying down with anybody. That was always her motto, business before pleasure. She looked at her reflection in the mirror as she pulled her hair up in a ponytail. Her phone vibrated loudly in the bedroom against the dresser. She rushed to it seeing Rico displayed on her cheap burner phone.

"Hello." said Lola dryly.

"Hello? What the fuck good?! You done fuckin' buckin' a nigga?" he shouted.

"What the fuck are you talkin' about?" said Lola defensively.

"I'm talkin' to you muhfucka. Been calling you for days now. I'm outside!"

"Yea, so what's that supposed to mean?"

"Come on Lo'. Stop bullshittin' bring yo' ass!"

"Yea" she pressed end on the screen ending the call. She walked over to Nana's room. It was empty she must've been at church, she pondered. Lola left her a note and headed outside. She saw Rico behind the wheel of a black Lexus. She smiled walking over to the passenger seat, climbing in. He looked her over, turning down the radio.

"So, what's good? What's with the buckin' and shit?"

Lola rolled her eyes.

"Ain't nobody buck you! I've been busy with Nan lately."

"You ain't ever been too busy for the crew before. What's up? Is it because of what popped off Friday?"

"Yea, what did pop off Friday?" said Lola folding her arms over her chest.

"Man, what didn't. He smiled. But no one fucked with you but some bitch Caesar called through."

"WHAT?"

Rico laughed.

"Yea, one of them hoes was loving your ass fucked up on the floor. She was goin' in on you, had me harder than a muhfucka! Ain't gon' lie."

"Y'all let some hoe eat my box! What kinda shit is that?" She hit him.

"You wasn't complaining. *Ooh! Ohhh!*   He mimicked her. So, we assumed your ass was good. Now you know if it was a nigga, I wouldn't have let that shit happen to you. He looked in her eyes. We good?"

"Yea, I bet Quan loved that shit."

"Every minute." said Rico a smile on his face. He put the car in drive speeding down the street.

She looked out the window looking at the passing cars. She saw a girl propped beside a candy apple red Lexus, Meika, decked out in bamboo earrings, thigh boots, cut off denim shorts and dashiki crop top. Meika was the around the way girl, every nigga sweated her but she fucked with the top dope boys only. She was brown skinned, thick hips and attitude. The light turned red, Rico looked over seeing her. "That bitch there fine as fuck."

Lola rolled her eyes. "What makes that bitch, so fine?"

"I mean her face ain't all that, but her body is badder than a muhfucka." She glanced at him.

"So, that's all that matters to a nigga is a bitch body?"

"I mean personally, I like a pretty bitch, freak, that can cook wit' a fat ass. That's wifey material. But a chic like Meika, is strictly fucking material." Lola shook her head.

"Thanks for enlightening me… that niggas petty ass fuck."

They arrived at the house. They went in through the back door down to the basement, is where they planned all their hits. She looked over seeing Quan and Caesar smoking a black & mild. Caesar smiled seeing Lola, she punched him in the arm. "What the fuck!" he shouted with a smirk on his face.

"You know why! I can't stand you Niggas!"

"You mad huh? Tighten up next time."

"Fuck you! I know your bitch ass started the shit." she said defensively. He stood up standing inches from her face. "You mad? What's good? Wanna throw hands?" He threw his hands in the air.

"You better get your punk ass out of my face."

"Or what my nigga? Caesar pointed his index finger in her face, I'm just saying don't come in here pissed and shit, because some bitch ate yo' box! Be more of a woman about yours, you slipped up!" She slapped Caesar across his face, he quickly palmed his cheek, before raising his hand to her face Rico jumped in between them. He grabbed Caesar's hand. "Yo! We not about to have this shit! I don't give a fuck I will blast both of y'all niggas. We got business to handle. Fuck this petty shit." Lola walked over to the table having a seat. Caesar massaged his cheek, still fuming as he sat down. "Now, we going to meet up around three tomorrow morning, me and Quan gonna be behind the truck, Lo gonna be in the S-Class, Caesar taking the Porsche. Quan gonna drive close to the truck and I'll get on and take the last one."

"What happened to taking the whole truck? Fuck that petty three car shit." said Caesar.

"It may be some cops out there because of that funeral. Cant fucking risk that shit." Caesar rolled his eyes.

"When we done, meet up on Moncrief, at eight. No mistakes in and out. We clear?" "Yea." said everyone in unison. Lola looked over to Caesar. His eyes gleamed with rage. She smiled. "Really Caes?"

"Fuck you, Lo. Don't say shit to me."

"Fuck you. Pussy ass nigga."

The next morning every one met up in the back of an abandoned building. Everyone dressed in black, Lola pinned her ponytail up in her hoodie. She placed her gloves over her hands, looking over to her crew. Her adrenaline racing thru her veins. *Let's do this shit!* She thought to herself. "A'ight. Everybody good?" said Rico. "Yea." They all replied. He looked around at them all. "A'ight. Let's go!"

They all piled into the car in minutes headed on 95 south. The music was blasting everyone was in war mode, passing a blunt around the car. Lola was never nervous, but today her nerves were on ten. But she could never turn her back on her crew. They had been through everything together. Rico looked at Lola through the rear view.

"Lo! You good back there?"

"Yeah, of course I am."

"A'ight. Don't front when this shit pop off."

"When do I ever? Save that speech for Caesar's punk ass." Caesar looked over to Lo cutting his eyes at her remark.

"If you got some dick in your life, you wouldn't be so worried about what the fuck I do."

Lola turned to him. "Do you want me to slap you again?"

"I'm just sayin. The only action we ever seen you have was a bitch eating your box. So what is it? You want pussy or dick?"

"I'm not a fucking dyke. From what I've heard you might as well be one, with that inch dick you got!" Rico and Quan in the front seat began to laugh. Caesar turned to Lola.

"Touch me. I want you to!" she taunted. Rico turned around. "Nah, we not having that shit! Focus, deal with that shit later. Let's get this money!"

Caesar turned away from Lola. Lola looked out the window saying a quick prayer. The car merged over to the rest area, pulling around to truck area. Lola slid her ski mask over her head. "A'ight. Remember the plan meet back up by eight." said Rico. Lola and Caesar crept out of the car, seeing the trailer a few feet away. Lola had her gun on her hip she looked up at the cars. Cease went around to check status on driver who was missing. Lambourghini, Ferrari, Maserati and Tesla, as well as Mercedes and a Porsche Cayenne. Lola approached the trailer first as Caesar made sure the coast was clear. Rico and Quan had pulled the car around front waiting on their departure. Lola broke into the lock box taking the key out before sliding behind the wheel. She looked around for Caesar, he was nowhere to be found. "Where the fuck is he?" The driver came around to the driver side of the truck and in minutes the truck was heading down the highway. Lola slid the key in ignition. The truck began to sway from side to side.

"What the fuck!" she screamed. She looked ahead and could see the driver side mirror and see that the driver was having a struggle. She rolled down the tinted window, a gunshot rang out in the night air.

"Hell no!" she put the car in reverse, flooring the pedal, the car went flying off the trailer. She looked around for Rico and Quan they were nowhere in sight. She could hear police sirens behind her. "Fuck! Think Lola! Think." She hit her hand on the steering wheel as she merged to the slow lane. She pulled beside the truck she could see Caesar and the driver fighting, another gunshot went off. She quickly merged over to the fast lane, reaching speeds of ninety five up the highway. She could see the truck in the rear view veer off to the side of the road. Cars began to crash into each other. She didn't have her phone. She didn't know what to do. She drove off into the morning dawn.

After driving several hours nonstop, she stopped in Valdosta, Georgia. She stopped by a gas station, she ran her fingers through her hair as she headed towards the bathroom in back of store. A young woman, no more than twenty stood by the rack of chips bending over choosing her selection. Lola noticed her cell sitting on the side of her purse. Lola clutched her stomach, before bumping into the woman. "Ohhh... my bad. Had too many drinks." The woman rolled her eyes before resuming picking her selections.

Lola walked into the stall unlocking the woman's phone. She decided to call Rico's phone. No answer. She called Quan's number. "Hello."

"Yo! What the fuck?"

"I told y'all it was a bad fucking move. Y'all should've bagged off."

"What the fuck are you talking about?"

"Lauren." said Quan. Lo looked at the phone in disbelief. She hung up abruptly. She powered the phone off placing it in her pocket paying for gas before leaving the store. Once on the highway she tossed the phone, heading towards Atlanta.

Exhausted, she checked in to the Hyatt Regency, downtown Peach Tree as she decided her next plan of action. Maybe she should buy a ticket to the West Coast? She could never go home, without having to fight and the way she felt now, she could kill Quan if she saw him. *Never snitch.* He broke all codes. She went over to the mirror taking off her hoody, she looked at her limp hair. Her clothes reeked of traveling and sweat. She needed some new clothes, first thing tomorrow. She laid on the bed pulling out all of the money she had. She had about five thousand dollars. How long would that get her over? She needed money, and a plan.

Florida Oranges & Georgia Peaches

She woke up the next morning took a shower and washed her hair. She left on her wife beater and jeans. She threw some money in her pockets and headed towards a mall. Thanks to the GPS system in the car she found the Lenox Square Mall without trouble. Her next plan would be to ditch the car. She stopped in Bebe, .not having a clue of what to purchase. Her sense of style was jeans, Timbs and a white tee. She walked over towards the jeans. A sales clerk stopped her.

"Hi may I help you?" Lola looked her up and down. She was a black woman, early twenties, about 5"7" brown eyes long brown hair wearing a pink sleeveless top and pencil skirt, and high heels. Makeup, long lashes and nicely manicured nails. She looked like one of those "high maintenance" girls that she despised. Mainly because they were everything she wasn't.

"Um... I'm good just looking for some jeans."

The girl looked her up and down.

"Okay. Our heartbreaker jeans would look great on you." she said with a smile. Lola half smiled at her, as the woman skimmed thru the jeans handing her a pair to look over. Lola held up the jeans seeing they were ripped skinny jeans. She cringed. She glanced over to the display seeing the jeans paired with nude bodysuits.

"So, what is your style?" Lola heard from behind. Normally, Lola would go off, but for some reason she was interested in what she wanted.

"What do you mean?" said Lola holding the jeans in her hand.

"Well, I'm just saying. Looking at you, you're pretty and all, but you dress like a butch. I know you're not a lesbian or stud."

Lola smiled. "Why am I not a lesbian?"

"Because I know you're not a lesbian! Besides you just need a makeover, this is not New York, this ATL and we don't wear Timbs in the summertime." Lola laughed aloud.

"Anyway, I do my own thing. I'm not trying to look like every other bitch. Timbs are all season."

The woman's demeanor shifted. "Well, anyway, my cousin is rapper Coodi and he is having a video release party at Rolex, I'm in charge of top notch ladies. So, maybe you can come through?"

"Why would I be interested in some shit like that? I'm good."

"Anyway, she walked over to the counter grabbing a flyer before walking back over. It's gonna be a lot of people out there, not just hoes, record execs and me too. My name is Brit. Give my name at the door."

"A'ight, Good to know." Lola slid the card into her back pocket.

She walked back over to the jean display. In walked two officers they began looking around. Lola looked out the corner of her eye as they came in her direction. *Shit!* Lola grabbed a few of the hideous bodysuits, pairs of jeans and two dresses that were on display. She walked briskly towards the register. A woman walked out the back over to the officers.

"I'm gonna get these."

"Oh okay, said Brit. You know you gonna need some shoes to go with that girl! We have an offer for a free pair of thong sandals right now. What size are you?"

"A size 7"

Brit grabbed a pair of jeweled flip flops adding on to her order. The cops stood by the door talking on their scanners with the woman.

"You should stop by Bloomies they have the perfect heels to go with this dress." Said Brit.

Lola looked over her shoulder to the cops, then back at Brit. "Will do." Replied Lola hastily. Brit sensed her urgency and quickly totaled the order. Lola reached in her pocket, peeling off a few hundred dollar bills. Once she received the change and bags she walked swiftly towards the exit. Lola headed towards Bloomingdales looking over her shoulder not seeing anyone following her. She let out a sigh of relief as she stopped by the MAC counter.

After spending over five hundred dollars on heels, makeup and a pair of sneakers, she decided it was time to go. She grabbed some fast food and stopped by a Target for hair dye and toiletries on her way back to the room. She looked at all the things she had brought. She picked up the hair dye, honey kissed blonde. She smirked. She thought she had picked up chestnut brown. With that run in with the cops at the mall was too close for comfort, she had to do something. She stood in the bathroom mirror and began on her hair. Hours later she looked at herself in the mirror she didn't recognize herself. She looked like a sexy china doll. The blond hair made her seductive slanted eyes pop. She pouted her lips in the mirror, giving her best sexy face. She dug in her bag looking for Brit's card about the party. It said it was tonight. She looked at her money, now she was short.

"Well, maybe there will be a few liks there." she said out loud with a smile on her face.

Around eleven o'clock, Lo arrived at the party. The line was wrapped around the building. All of the girls were scantily clad and half naked. Ass everywhere. Valet parked her car and she stepped up to the red carpet all eyes went to her. She fixed the dress strap. The bouncers at the door stared at her curves.

"Damn, she thick" Lola was wearing a black Bebe bandage dress that showed every curve. Her breasts were sitting like mounds; her honey skin glistened with her blonde hair. Her round ass and long legs, commanded all eyes on her as she sauntered over to the front of the line.

"How can I help you?"

"I'm here with... um Brit?"

"Okay... what's your name?"

"Lo." He got on the walkie and in minutes Brit came to the door. Lola barely recognized her, once pinned up tresses was now a Chinese bang and long black straight hair. She had on a lace jeweled black corset top and spandex boy shorts and black strappy Christian Louboutin's on her feet. "Hey! You came! Look at you!"

"Yea, said Lola, pulling down her dress.

"Come!" she grabbed her hand pulling her into the club. She looked around the party. Liquor bottles were everywhere, dancing half naked girls as the music vibrated the floor. Brit led her upstairs to VIP. Goons all around, Lola was skeptical. *Damn, I should've bought my piece.* She thought to herself but where would she had put it. Brit led her over to a table in back where two women were seated. One was light skinned, sexy the other was brown skinned with an ice grill plastered to her face. She flipped her hair over her shoulder looking down in her phone.

"These are my girls Vita, she pointed to the light skinned girl and this is Nika."

"What up! Said Vita with a heavy Nuyorican accent.

"What's your name?" Said Brit.

"Lo." Nika excused herself from the table. Lola looked over her outfit; she was wearing a v neckline, black mini dress that barely covered her round ass. She had a "badonk" that you could sit a drink on, but her face wasn't pretty at all to Lo.

"Have a seat." said Vita. Lo walked around the booth to sit down. She glanced over at Nika who was in the arms of a man with all black on.

"What's her problem?" said Lo.

"What you mean?" said Brit.

"That bitch, looking at me sideways. She doesn't know me. I am not the one."

"Well, I don't know you either. But, you seemed like a cool bitch." said Brit with a smile. Vita laughed.

"Don't mind Brit she a bit fucked up already. She can't hold her fuckin' liquor. Don't mind Nika, I barely fuck wit' her ass either." Lo smiled. Vita looked towards the direction of the men. "See all of those niggas in that booth over there, she pointed to the right, those are some of Atlanta's biggest hustlers, ya feel me." Lola looked slightly over, trying to be discreet.

"That's Bunk, Los, Mill and Uno. Bunk, the low key nigga don't let it fool you crazy as hell. Heard he's a down low nigga, crazy paper. Los second nigga in charge, he owns a lot of the strip clubs here, Latino nigga, good dude. Mill, sexy, the enforcer, will lay a bitch out at drop of a dime. Uno is the boss, got bread out the ass, owns restaurants, dealerships, record labels and shit. Trini nigga, sexy as hell but nigga definitely got bodies under his belt. Feel me?" Lo looked over at Uno. He was brown skinned, low cut, thick brows, bright wide almond eyes, and his presence commanded attention out of the group. Wearing a v neck black shirt, Hermes belt and black pants and loafers. Thick beard with a toned build, he was definitely eye candy. Lo turned back to Vita.

"So why are you telling me this?"

"Just letting you know. Brit always picks top notch bitches for her wack ass cousin, but hoes always come and go straight for the source. You don't seem like you about games. So I figured I'd cut out the bullshit."

"Okay, and which nigga is yours?" said Lo.

"How you know one of them mine?"

"Because, I know game and no bitch gonna give a hoe stats on the niggas in here with the most bread." Vita smiled.

"I like you. Mill"

She looked over at Mill; he was wearing a black long sleeve shirt, jeans and Timbs. He was dark skinned about six feet tall. His hair was cut low. Brit got up, falling out of her funk.

"I'm going to get Coodi okay."

"A'ight. Whateva." said Vita. Lo glanced back to the baller table. Uno locked eyes with her. She quickly looked away. When she glanced over again, he was still staring at her. Vita stood up.

"Come on, let's get a drink." Lola looked over Vita's outfit she was wearing a black lace dress which looked more like a negligee. As the strobe flashed over them, Lola was able to take in Vita's flawless appearance as she walked beside her. Her honey skin, wand black curls down her back, DD breast, slender waist and "badonk ass" she was wearing stiletto heels, the point was ridiculously narrow. She walked as if she was gliding across the floor. They stepped over to the bar, Vita ordered them two tequila shots a piece. As she took a shot she took a little box out of her dress, which resembled an Altoid box.

"You want? said Vita as she opened the box placing a few of the contents on her tongue. "Nah, I'm good."

Lo looked around taking in the scene, the music was blasting. Vita soon began dancing. She bent over making her ass clap to the music. Lo looked away, feeling awkward, a part of her wishing she was free as Vita was. In minutes, Mill had come over to the bar.

"Pull that shit down. Before, I slap the shit outta you!" Lo turned slightly seeing him standing beside Vita, his hand clenched around the back of her neck.

"I'm having a good fucking time a'ight. You brought me to this shit, so me and Lo is gonna have a good fuckin' time!" she shouted belligerently. He looked over to Lo. Lola side eyed Vita.

"Who you?"

"That's my home girl Lo! Why?" said Vita. He looked over Lo's dress which was as tight as Vita's. He looked back into Vita's eyes.

"Get yo shit together V, he said tightening the grip on her neck, show your ass again. See what the fuck I do!" said Mill angrily in her ear, which could be heard over the music.

She smiled sweetly. She looked into his eyes as she placed her manicured hand on his chest. "I want you so bad right now baby." She kissed his lips. He put his arm around her body.

"You ready, now huh? Let's go." He kissed her lips.

"Lo… I'll be back. Unless you wanna…"

"Nah I'm cool." Moments later they were gone and Lo walked back over to the table. As she sat alone, she began to rethink her original plan. She took in the whole scene, thinking about her situation. She was wondering how her nana was doing, and the status of her crew. She wished she was in Jacksonville right now. She sighed, leaning back in the booth. When she looked back forward she saw a gold letter H belt in her face.

"What's good beautiful?" She looked up seeing Uno in front of her. Now in her face she could really see him, he was sexy. Tattoos covered his arms, she immediately noticed his West Indian accent. His diamond chain glistened along with his bright white smile.

"Hey." said Lo, immediately displaying an ice grill on her face.

"What's your name?"

"Lo."

"A'ight, Lo, who are yuh here with?"

"I came with Brit." said Lo adjusting herself in the booth.

"Who is that?" he replied disgusted.

"Brit...her cousin... Coodi having a party?"

"I don't know that nigga. Anyway, this party was for my nigga, Los. So, yuh gonna offer me a seat or what?" He said with a certain level of cockiness.

"I guess, since it is your nigga party, you can sit wherever you want." She moved over to allow him to sit down. He pulled up his pants as he sat in the seat.

"So where yuh from?" said Uno looking directly into her eyes.

"Florida."

"What part?" He replied with a smile on his face.

"Tampa. She blurted out quickly. Have you been there before?"

"I been through there a couple of times. But, we can cut all this small talk here and I can talk to yuh about that over breakfast."

"What you mean, breakfast?" said Lola with an attitude. He laughed.

"I like breakfast. Besides we can hit up Lenox, see what yuh about. So, give me your number and I can hit yuh up." Lo crossed her legs. Somewhat, entertained by his aggressive charm. "I don't have a phone."

Uno leaned his back up against the booth, looking over to her. "Yuh serious?"

"Dead ass." she replied sharply.

"Why don't yuh have a phone? If I may ask."

"I just haven't had a chance to get a new one."

She looked back into his eyes.

"Can't have that, hold up. He got on his phone, his accent was more noticeable. Lo looked him over reading his body language. He had a simple diamond bracelet on his tattooed wrist, clean nails and she saw a tattoo on his neck but couldn't make out what it said in the darkness of club. In minutes he was off the phone.

Lo glanced at the others around the club when she looked back in front of her there was a white woman standing beside the table with a briefcase. Lo became guarded.

"Hi, Mr. Uno, you needed a new phone right?" said the woman.

"Yea for her."

The woman was cute, late thirties, prim and proper wearing a pencil skirt and red button down shirt. She opened the suitcase and inside were boxes from top carriers. She pulled out two boxes an iPhone 8 plus and a Samsung Note 8. Which would you like? I can get the iPhone in any color for you. I brought gold and space gray. Lo whose last phone was just a cheap burner didn't care to ever upgrade to a smart phone, was overwhelmed.

"Um... I don't... Lo started.

Uno interjected. "Give her the gold one."

"Okay, I'll have it going immediately. You need light case for it? Ring light? Beats headphones? Certain area code you need?"

"No on code and okay sure." said Lo agreeing she couldn't believe this was happening. The woman began taking the paper off the screen and activating the phone.

"Why are you doing this?" asked Lo.

"Because, yuh don't have a phone and if I want to talk to yuh, it seems this is the only way that's gonna happen right?"

"Yea, but what do you think this is gonna act as a tracking device? I'm not with that."

"I don't need a phone for that." He replied looking into her eyes.

The woman handed Lo the phone. "Here you are lovely. You are all set." She jotted the new number down on a business card placing it on the table

"Appreciate it, Karen."

"Pleasure is mine." She packed up her briefcase and in moments was out of sight. Lo looked down at the phone, it displayed the time brightly. The phone began to ring loudly, she looked at the screen unsure of what to do.

"Go ahead and lock me in. I got to head out, but look forward to seeing yuh at breakfast today."

"A'ight. We'll see, I'm not a morning person."

"A'ight, holla at yuh." He touched her leg before exiting the table. Some of his men approached him and they headed towards the back. Lo was ready to leave. Vita came back over to the table plopping down.

"Hey Lo, You good?"

"Yea, are you?" Lo looked over her body she reeked of sex and alcohol.

"Yea had to handle that real quick before he gets on my nerves tomorrow." She pulled out a mirror fixing her hair. She looked over to Lo's phone on the table.

"Yo you have the eight plus?! I was going to get this one. Let me get your number Lo so we can chill." said Vita.

"Hell, I don't even know the number, I just got it."

"Call my number and lock it in."

Vita recited her number as Lola saved it to her contacts.

"How about tomorrow, we go get our hair and nails done?"

"I'm not into that."

"Being a top notch, you gotta stay on top. Just like you came in tonight, new pussy is always lurking. So, tomorrow I scoop you up?"

"Yea, alright." said Lo.

"Well, let's go. This is over." Vita got up and Lo followed her out thru the crowds of people. Eyes followed as they glided thru the room. Not one man touched. When they reached the parking lot, Vita headed towards a Black BMW.

"Talk to you later chica, a'ight" She shouted at Lo. "Alright" Lo went to her car and headed to the hotel. Still replaying all that transpired tonight a part of her curious about Uno, he had definitely peaked her interest.

When she arrived to her room she was exhausted. She stripped off her dress throwing on a white Hanes tee she had picked up from store earlier, plopping down in the bed in seconds sleeping. The next morning around nine o'clock her phone rang. She looked at the screen, Uno. She smiled, wiping her eyes, sitting up. "Hello."

"Good morning Lo." He replied his voice warm. "What's up?" she replied yawning.

"Me and yuh breakfast. You down?"

"Right now? I haven't showered yet."

"A'ight. Well, shower and meet me at South City Buckhead at ten."

"Really?"

"Yes, I'm serious." he said certain.

"Alright."

"See yuh soon." She hung up the phone getting up to shower. Afterwards, she looked through the bags of things she had bought. All she had was jeans and those bodysuits, she looked over her shoe choices sandals or the heels from last night. She threw on a pair of the ripped blue jeans, and the white lace up bodysuit. She looked at her ass in the mirror, the jeans fit like a glove, she didn't like it, but decided fuck it what else could she wear. Lola quickly brushed her teeth and applied lip gloss to her lips. She called down to have a cab pick her up, before heading down.

Once she arrived to the restaurant and paid the driver she looked at the door there was two men standing guard outside of restaurant, she stared at them. The parking lot seemed bare. They moved out the way to let her through. She walked into the restaurant, seeing it was empty. The waiter led her to the back. The restaurant upscale yet rustic chic. Uno appeared seated wearing a black Polo shirt and matching shorts. In the daylight, Uno looked completely different. Handsome and rugged. His eyes were dark chestnut brown and doe shaped, his skin milk chocolate, charming white smile and his body was towering. He smiled seeing her.

"Good morning." He stood up to greet her. She hugged him. "Morning." She replied. He glanced over her ass then at her face as they embraced.

"What are you mixed with?"

"I'm Thai and Trini."

"Trini gyal huh? I like of course." he sipped his orange juice.

"You are Trini?"

"Yea, don't act like yuh didn't know by my accent." He said with a smile. The waitress brought her a mimosa. She sipped it slowly. "Well, Lo I like what I see. I don't fuck around, ya know. I want to get to know yuh, spoil yuh, fuck yuh… all dat shit." Lo almost spit out her drink. She was not prepared for his bluntness.

"Well, I'm not about being a fuck." said Lo looking into his eyes.

"I'm not looking for yuh to be a fuck, I want to get to know yuh, build with yuh. Feel me?" Soon two waiters came back with their food. It was waffles, bacon, eggs and grits along with frittatas, which he had already ordered. She always hated waffles for some reason. But she didn't want to be rude. The waiters left. She looked over to his plate, it was spilling over with meat. He looked up feeling her watching him.

"Got enough food?" said Lo.

"Well, breakfast is the most important meal of the day right."

"That's what they say. But, I've never been big on breakfast." She began to mix bacon with her grits.

"So tell me about yuh Lo. What brought yuh to Atlanta?" She cleared her throat.

"Um, wanting something new." She replied quickly.

"Something new, huh? So yuh like spur of the moment shit? Jet setting shit?"

"I mean, I wouldn't say I'm a jetsetter. But, when my mind is set I go with it." She wiped her mouth. The pecan bacon was everything, she thought of ordering an order to go.

"I hear that. I'm going to Cali in two days. I want yuh to come with me."

"What?!" she replied shocked.

"Yea I have a few business things to handle. But, I wanna spend some time with yuh." He looked in her eyes.

"I don't know you! No offense, you could be crazy or some shit! What makes you think I'm gonna go clear across the country with you?"

"Because in two days, you'll be calling me your fuckin' boo." A smile formed across his lips. His perfect possibly porcelain smile, she couldn't help but smile at his confidence. Her phone began to ring. Startled, she looked for the phone in her back pocket. It was Vita.

"Hello."

"Yo, Lo. It's Vita. What's up mami?"

"Hey. What's going on?"

"Me and you are going to the salon to get our shit layed."

"Well, um…" Uno smiled at her. "It's all good. Yuh can go chill wit' her." Lo looked at her. *How did he know it was a female?* She then realized the volume was loud anyone could hear it was a female.

"Okay, well let me finish breakfast and I'll meet you at Lenox Square."

"A'ight. See you there." She ended the call placing the phone on the table. Uno looked at her. "So you going to chill with your home girl?"

"We're going to get our hair and nails done, I guess."

He looked at her nails. They were chipped and looked as if they had never been painted in her life. He reached under the table, placing a Hermes Bolide leather bag on top of the table. He slid it over to her.

"I was gonna take you out, show you around. But, I guess I'll see you at dinner."

"Are you asking me on another date?" she replied folding her arms across her chest.

"I noticed yuh didn't have one. Take the contents and get yourself all sexied up and I'll come scoop yuh later. She hesitantly picked up the bag. Don't worry, there's more where that came from. If yuh stay on this team." Uno got up from the table. He walked over to her side of the table, he kissed her cheek walking out the door. Lo looked across the table seeing he left a hundred dollar bill on the table. She placed the bag on her arm heading out the door. She called a cab to pick her up and take her to the mall. As she sat in the backseat she opened the bag skimming over the contents. The bag was filled with hundred dollar bills. It was over ten thousand dollars. *What the fuck!* She said out loud, She had never gotten this much money from a man! Is this all it took? Maybe she had it all wrong years ago, when she was one of the guys stealing cars. She smiled looking at the money. *I am not mad at you hoes* .She thought.

Her phone rang interrupting her thoughts

"Where are you?"

"I'm outside in the parking lot."

"I'll meet you outside Louis Vuitton." She walked into the mall, not having a clue where Louis Vuitton was, she looked on the guide on a pole.

"Really Bitch?!" she heard loudly behind her. She realized it was Vita. Vita was beautiful. She looked completely different in the morning light. Her flowing black curls rested on her shoulder and down her back. She was wearing a nude crop top and matching pencil skirt. Nude Christian Louboutin pumps on her feet. Diamond studs in her ear and a diamond rosary around her neck, Cartier watch on her wrist. Her face was makeup free but she was beautiful to Lo, she looked like a Latina goddess. Vita hugged her.

"How are you?" said Vita.

"I'm alright, a little tired."

"Girl, me too. But, I gotta get myself right. Can't be out here looking like a bum bitch. Said Vita, half seriously. So, I hear Uno got his eyes on you."

Lo stopped in her tracks, "how do you know?"

"My man is his nigga. He was asking me about you. I'm like I barely know her, but she seem like cool people. So, I'm gonna fuck with you, ya know." People stared at them as they walked through the mall. Vita didn't pay them any attention.

"Well, we went out to breakfast this morning. He seems alright. Hella cocky and aggressive."

"Uno, is a good dude. Although he doesn't say too much, I know he will definitely take care of you. My one piece of advice, watch everyone who you talk to around that nigga. Because, he has Atlanta on lock! Anybody you associate with best believe he will know."

"What are you saying, I'm to be scared or some shit?" said Lo defensively.

"No. Just don't associate with lame niggas. You're a top notch pretty bitch. When you start getting known throughout the city, people gonna look at you as a threat. I don't see any bitch as a threat. But, you got some simple hoes out there that's gonna want your spot, always remember that."

"Just because I have a pretty face, doesn't mean I'm gonna take shit. People don't know me or my story. I'm more than a pretty face."

Vita laughed. "Yea that you are. A pretty face that's been in bad need of a makeover."

Lo laughed." Fuck you!"

"Now you're speaking my language that I like!" said Vita in her best Scarface impression.

Hours later they were heading to the salon. Each of them had bags galore, they took Vita's car. Vita's car was a Black BMW 745. Big rims and had black and pink leather seats. Vita opened the trunk to place the bags inside. Lo put hers on the side, she had never went shopping like this before. A surge of adrenaline filled her veins. Vita got behind the wheel, she pulled out a tiny altoid box.

"You want?"

"I'm good." said Lo.

"A'ight suit yourself. She took a few out placing them in her mouth downing them with water. Vita turned the radio up blasting, T.I. She zoned out as they headed to a salon in Bankhead. Lo realized this must be the hood.

"We are now in the hood! They do the best hair out here."

"Really."

"Yea. I made an appointment, so it's only us in here today." Vita pulled into the parking lot. To a black brick building, two stories with gold columns outside. They walked inside and two stylists were sitting in the chairs. One was a man, Dante' and the other a woman, Yani. Dante was cute thin, black with a black Mohawk. He was wearing a button down shirt tucked in a pair of white polo khakis with a baby blue bowtie. Yani was brown skinned, wearing a maxi dress and her hair was in a top knot.

"What's good Vita? What can I do for you today?"

"My regular. Wash, curl and can you have Shandi for my mani pedi." She walked over to Yani's chair sitting down.

"What about your friend?" said Dante' looking Lo up and down.

"Oh, that's Lo. The fabulous Dante'. Tell him what you want."

"Well I just want to curl this, I guess maybe some layers." Dante' came over running his fingers through her thick wavy hair. "Ooh, you have a beautiful hair texture. Bad, choice of color boo. What is this a rinse?" He threw his hand up disgusted. Lo looked confused.

"What else you need a mani, pedi, hmmm… wax?"

"What you trying to say?"

"I'm only asking a question boo. Don't pop off." he said with his hand on his hip.

"Well, when I feel I'm being insulted I can act however the fuck I want." everyone looked at Lo.

"Dante', chill out a'ight? She's new!" Dante' rolled his eyes. Lo sat down.

Four hours later it was going on five. Lo had a brand new mani and pedi, eyebrow wax and her hair was almost finished. He turned her to the mirror. Her hair was now a platinum blonde. The way he feathered the curl around her face drew you to her eyes. It was long, curly and sexy. The body her hair now had was amazing she felt she looked like a model on the cover of a magazine.

"This is amazing. I don't know who I am!" Vita got up from the chair.

"That is fly! The new and improved top notch bitches we are." Lo laughed looking at herself in the mirror. Vita's black hair looked healthy and was loosely curled. Vita handed Yani four hundred dollars. Lo went into her new bag.

"How much?" "It will be four fifty, for everything." Lo handed Dante the cash. Before heading out the door. Lo's phone rang, she knew it was Uno. She smiled.

"Hello."

"What up. You ready for dinner?"

"I will be, where are we going?"

"Meet me at the Chateau in Buckhead. In about an hour, I have some business to handle real quick."

"Okay. See you there." Lo hung up placing the phone in her purse.

"That Uno?"

"Yea, were going out to dinner."

"Oh okay. He's known for his set times of the day."

"What do you mean?"

"I've heard that he's very punctual and shit like that."

"Oh. Okay."

"Where do you live?"

"Well, I'm in a hotel right now. Haven't decided if Atlanta is the place for me, ya know?"

"Let me tell you, all niggas with money come thru here. Not even that, you can be your own fucking boss bitch here. Just depends on how you play your position, feel me? But first order of business, you gotta get a place baby doll, out in the cut. If you plan on continuing to hang with Uno that's gotta be step one."

"I don't have a job, I've never had a job." said Lo.

"Neither have I. But, I live in Buckhead. Three car garage, four bedroom house, never worked a day in my life."

"How old are you?" said Lo.

"I'm twenty five. No kids, two abortions and I'm ahead of the game. You"

"I'm twenty one. Just trying to find me, ya know."

"Baby girl, you have so much learning to do. You can have anything in this world you want, if you go out and get it." Lo smiled thinking of her past thievery. She immediately thought of the crew. She wondered what everyone was doing right now and how was nana. Her thoughts quickly began to race with thoughts of guilt. She shook the thoughts out of her mind. Vita pulled out her mint box popping a few in her mouth.

"So, I'm supposed to meet him at the Chateau in Buckhead. I don't know where that is."

"Oh that's not that far, from where you were. Better yet it's close to my crib, we can get you a car service and you can get dressed at my place."

"Okay. That's cool." Lo looked out the window.

Thirty minutes later she was at Vita's beautiful home. If she never worked a day in her life maybe Lo could definitely take pointers from her. The house was spacious yet warm and cozy with its white room and bling decor throughout the house. In the foyer there was a wall size painting of Vita standing on a beach. The kitchen granite counter tops, mirrors everywhere with porcelain tile all the way through. Vita sat at the bar taking off her heels. Vita showed her over to the guest room and bathroom. Lo pulled out what she purchased, she took a quick shower. She decided on a black Herve Leger bandage cocktail dress. Her back was completely exposed, the dress fit her every curve. Paired with Giuseppe Zanotti patent leather peep toe heels. She sprayed Dolce & Gabbana "The One" perfume on her neck.

"How do I look, Vi?" Lo came out in front of her spinning around. A proud smile came across her face.

"Yasss slay bitch!"

Lola laughed out loud. "I guess that means I did good?"

"Hell yea! I told you that you just needed a little help. But, you're gorgeous honey. You have some nice legs too!" Vita walked over. Those earrings are all wrong though. Hold on. Vita went into her room and brought out a pair of Gold chandelier earrings. Put these on. Let me do your makeup."

Lo pulled out the makeup they had bought from Sephora and Mac. When Vita was done fifteen minutes later, Lo looked at herself in the mirror she couldn't believe her eyes. She was flawless, the contour was everything, and she couldn't help but smile at her reflection. The red lipstick and bronzed cheeks along with the eyeliner made her slanted eyes stand out.

"Wow. V, who is this girl! I've never looked like this my whole life."

"Aww," Lo hugged her gently.

"Oh shit, I better go! Thanks for everything Vita, I'll call you tomorrow okay."

"A'ight Girl! Have fun." Lo rushed out the door as she rushed out in the driveway. She looked up to see Mill getting out of a Mercedes walking her way. He looked her up and down, not believing his eyes. "Hi, she replied to his stares.

"What up. What's your name?"

"Lo. You're Mill right? I met you last night."

"Yea, okay."

"Sorry, I'm in a rush. Nice meeting you though." said Lo realizing she sounded like a complete "girly girl." He looked at her ass as it bounced as she hurried to the car. He turned away going inside.

Ten minutes later, she arrived at Chateau. The waiter took her to the back entrance of the restaurant like before. Everyone's eyes followed her as she walked through. When they reached the table, Uno's back was to her. As the waiter announced her presence, he turned around seeing Lo. He smiled taking in her beauty. He stood up from the table to hug her. He held her tightly in his arms briefly palming her derriere. Lo smiled. He smelled good and looked even better. He was wearing a black button down shirt and a pair of dark jeans possibly Gucci. He had a diamond necklace on his neck, diamond watch and bracelet.

"Damn! Yuh look good as fuck tonight, I can't even front."

"Thank you." she replied with a coy smile.

"Yuh have a good time shopping with your girl?"

"We did alright. Good times."

"Alright. So, yuh gave my trip invitation anymore thought?"

"Yea, I have, I'm still thinking about it."

"Alright, that's good, there is still a chance." He smiled. The waiter came back with a bottle of Belaire Rosé. Lo sat back trying to take in this moment, as butterflies fluttered in the pit of her stomach. An hour later, Lo had a slight buzz and she was playing twenty questions with Uno, trying to learn more about him.

"So, how old are you? You have a woman?"

"27 and no,"

"Kids?" said Lo.

"Nope" He sipped from his glass never losing his gaze with her.

"What about yuh?"

"21 and no." His phone buzzed. He looked at the screen, and then placed it in his pocket.

"I gotta go by a spot real quick."

"Oh, ok." He got up from the table. Lo stood up adjusting her dress and trying to grab her purse quickly. Uno led the way to the back entrance where his car was parked. It was a black Maserati with black rims. He walked around opening her door. Lo got in smelling the familiar smell of weed and black & mild's. She immediately thought of Rico a smile came to her face. Uno got behind the wheel speeding off down the road. The sounds of Popcaan blasting thru the speakers. Uno looked over to her, he placed his hand on her leg. In moments they were at the rear of a club. Security open the doors escorting them inside a side entrance. Uno extended his hand which she cuffed his arm instead as they walked thru the doors and to elevator doors which led up to an office. Club goers in the hall gawked over Lola's revealing dress, wanting to know who she was and why she was on his arm. When they arrived at the office you could see three men sitting inside. He looked over to Lo.

"Ma, go out to my table and I'll be out there in a second."

"Okay."

He touched her arm gently. "Tell them bring yuh bottles. Whatever you want." Lo walked away realizing once again she didn't know where she was going. She ended back by the security guard. "I need to get to Uno's table."

"Right this way." He said jumping to her order. He led her to the door that went into V.I.P. It overlooked the entire club. It had a pool table, personal bar and television that covered an entire wall. The booth was comfortable and sat about six. A bartender walked over to Lo with a black bottle. "Thank you." said Lo.

"You're welcome. Would you like anything else; Food, massage or a request for DJ?"

"Um... No thank you." Lo went over to the window overlooking the dance floor. She looked down seeing the women on poles dancing as men threw money at them. *A strip club.* She shook her head walking back to the booth. She sipped the wine and began toying with her earring bored.

"Hola Bitch!" someone screamed from across the room. She realized it was Vita, dressed flawlessly in a white jumpsuit that was sheer on one side revealing her whole left side. Sophia Webster lace and satin booties and her hair was braided on one side and her long curly locks flowed freely on the other.

"Hey V! What are you doing here?"

"Girl, this is the discussion spot. They always have a discussion before trips. The Cali trip coming up. I normally don't go, but I want to hit up Rodeo and get some new shit."

"So you guys are going too?" said Lo.

"Yea, Mill is definitely going. Anytime, Uno is on the road, Mill is there. Why did he ask you to go?"

"Yea. I didn't know about going yet, ya know."

"Girl, you better come! We can go shopping and hit up L.A. clubs! You will love it. You have to go. Private jet!"

"What?"

"You're gonna go in a private jet. I'm going first class. They normally split up and fly in, separately, but, we will definitely meet up."

"A'ight. I guess I will go." Vita smiled.

"Why you cooped up here? Come on lets go downstairs." Lo got up, following Vita's lead downstairs. The security guard followed behind them. Lo turned around.

"Are you following me?"

"Yes. I am to make sure you're safe while in here. Direct orders." Vita touched Lo's shoulder. "It's okay."

Downstairs, Lo looked around the room. She saw half naked women everywhere. Pool tables, bars and an aquarium inside the bar. Men's eyes soon followed them, many noticing security with them stating they were off limits.

Vita led Lo to the dance floor. She began to rock her hips as she threw her hands in the hair. Moving seductively on Lo. Lo not too much of a dancer moved stiffly side to side. Vita laughed. "What the hell are you doing girl? All that ass. You better move that shit!"

Lo laughed. "I'm not a dancer."

"Yes, you are. Vita placed her hands on Lo's hips. Rock from side to side like this. Vita began to move slowly from side to side, her hair swaying against her ass as she grinded slowly. Lo began to mimic her moves. She arched her back and began to move her hips from side to side. Vita smiled proudly. You got it! Move your hands like this up and down your body. Vita began to touch herself, as she ran her fingers in her hair. Niggas love that shit. Lo began to let loose and in minutes they had an audience. Guys began to throw money at them. Vita bent down looking at the ones.

"Seriously? Keep this shit! I need real money!!" Lo laughed. Someone touched Lo's arm.

"What's good ma?" Lo turned around seeing a brown skinned man, about five foot ten, wearing all black and Yankee fitted. "Umm... Hi." said Lo half embarrassed.

"Dame"

"Um... Lo." He shook her hand. "You sexy as hell, baby." Vita realized Lo's awkward encounter. She pulled Lo to the side.

"Look if you plan on kicking it with Uno don't talk to these lames in his spot."

"Huh? I wasn't ..."

"I know it's all fun and you had a few drinks. But, they don't see it that way. Remember once you are seen with Uno, according to the streets y'all are together. You feel me? I got your back but, I thought I should school you to this game."

"I got you." said Lola. They began to walk away.

"Besides, you don't wanna waste time talking to that corner crab nigga. Why fuck with him and you can be fucking with the boss?" said Vita laughing. Lola smiled at her. Vita seemed to know all the rules to the game. Lola decided to follow her lead, and maybe she could learn a few things. Because she hadn't had a clue.

Fancy

Days later, around three in the morning, Lola was packing her bags for the Los Angeles trip. Vita had assured her they would have a good time together and would probably only see the guys at night, which was cool with her. She began to love Vita's companionship. Lola had decided to listen to Vita's advice and find a place when they returned so this would be her final checkout. Vita offered that she could store some of her clothes in one of her garages. Lo agreed being she didn't have too many things besides clothes. She placed the final things in her bag, which was a DVF carry-on bag she found at a retail store. She rolled the bag beside the door, leaving to her car. Uno was to pick her up from the lobby. She had scoped out in recent days wooded areas around town. She found a nice wooded area, by the Lenox mall, which was a hill which led to a nice open cul de sac in the center. It wasn't the best place, but she realized she better do this now or never.

She had been spending a lot of time with Uno and didn't want anything to go down with the car. She lit a match to the seat watching the car soon go up in flames. As the car burned she reminisced of her crew. The flame became intense Lola backed up darting off into the woods. She called a cab and in minutes later was back at the hotel. When the cab pulled up to the hotel she saw, a red Range Rover, pull up behind it. She looked at the rims, and knew this had to be Uno. The passenger window rolled down.

"You ready?" She walked over to the window.

"Yea, I just have to go upstairs real quick to get my bag."

"Alright." she walked into the hotel and moments later returned with her bags. She placed them in the backseat climbing in the front seat with Uno. He smiled seeing her. "How yuh doing beautiful?"

"I'm okay. How are you?"

"I'm good." He replied firing up his blunt. He pulled away from the curb speeding off down the street.

"So, why were you getting out of a cab?"

"Oh, I had to go to Walgreens real quick to pick up feminine things ya know."

"Yuh have a car?"

"No."

"hmm…" Lola didn't know what was with all the questions, but she was happy to have answered them without hesitation. Vita had schooled her on how Uno could always tell a liar. He was known to have hated liars. She smiled, but this little white lie couldn't hurt.

They arrived at the airport minutes later. There was a jet waiting on the runway. Lola didn't want to look like an excited little girl, but she was. She had never been on a plane, and now she was going to be on a private plane heading to Los Angeles. She smiled as the driver opened her door. Another came to get her luggage. Uno was on his phone, he looked back at her.

"Come on, baby." He replied with a warm smile. Once on the plane an attendant brought her out a glass of wine, she looked at the furniture in awe. Uno went over to the table to have a seat, he pulled out his MacBook Lo laid back on the recliner. The attendant came back.

"Would you like a mani or pedi or massage?"

"Umm…"

"She'll take them all." said Uno. Lo smiled.

"I guess I'll take them all." Uno ended his phone call.

"Stay on my team, baby… I'll show yuh the world." He smiled.

Hours later they were in Los Angeles. She looked out the window, there was a black Bentley continental waiting on the runway. *What the fuck! This is the life.* She thought. She messaged Vita. *"I'm here bitch!"*

She looked over to Uno he was sleeping; she sat on top of his lap. She spoke softly in his ear. "We're here." He awoke a smile on his face.

"Damn! Don't do that baby, make me wanna fuck yuh right here." She smiled. He wrapped his arms around her body kissing her neck.

"So, when I'm gonna get to see all of this naked?" He placed his hands under her shirt caressing her back.

"Sooner than later." she replied with a mischievous grin on her face.

"A'ight, that's what I wanna hear." She removed herself from his lap. He grabbed a Louis Vuitton bag on the floor. He handed it to her.

"Here this is for you, while you're here. Make sure yuh get plenty of shit I like, and Vita should be here soon. I know y'all about to do some girl shit."

"Wait, so how am I gonna get around?"

"I got yuh a driver; don't worry everything is already taken care of." A black Yukon pulled up beside the Bentley.

"You can take the Bentley. See yuh at dinner a'ight?" "Okay." She kissed his cheek. She looked over to the Bentley the driver was waiting outside. They exited the plane to their separate cars.

The driver opened the back door to let Lo inside. She smiled seeing champagne chilled in the back. First class. Her phone chimed it was Vita.

"Just touchdown. Where are you?"

"At the airport. I'll come get you." She texted back a smiling face emoji. She had the driver to go to Vita's terminal. She looked up to see Vita dressed flawlessly like always. She could make the simplest outfit look fly. She was wearing light blue skinny jeans that had rips at the knees and hugged her every curve. A sleeveless shirt which was grey which read diamonds are a girl's best friend. Her hair in a top knot and a Chanel bag on her arm. The driver opened the door to let her in.

"Welcome to LA Bitch!" Lola screamed at her.

Vita hugged her. "Welcome? You just got here too trick." They both laughed. Lola looked at her black spiked heels.

"I love your shoes."

"Giuseppe's, of course."

"Cute. So, where you want to go?" said Lo.

"Girl, let's eat. Hit up some stores."

"Sounds like a plan to me." An hour and a half later they were heading to Chanel. Lola decided to look in the bag that Uno had given her. As she quickly unzipped the bag bundles of money came falling out.

"What the fuck!" she screamed. Vita looked at the money covering her lap.

"Uno."

"Yes... Where the fuck am I gonna spend all of this"

"I can tell you a few places." said Vita sarcastically.

"I can't believe he gave me all this."

"Lo, believe it. You are about to be Miss Uno! Atlanta is going to be yours and you are about to have everything!"

"I mean this is crazy. I haven't fucked him or anything, Vi. What the fuck?! I mean I definitely feel there is some chemistry there. I am feeling him."

"Well, better get to fucking."

Lola laughed loudly. "Well, he told me to get a lot of sexy things he would like."

"Well, I can help you with that. But, what you should definitely do is put some aside for your place. So, when you get back your set. First, piece of advice mama is always keep a little stashed away every time he hits you up with dough. Always stay too steps ahead of him and have money for a rainy day. Ya feel me?"

"Yea. I got you. So, let's hit up Agent Provocateur and get you a few sexy pieces." "Okay." The first stop was a boutique Vita loved. Vita walked over to the shoes and Lola followed. As the employee came over to help she began handing shoes to her. "Size 7."

Lola picked up shoes and tried them on her feet. Deciding if she liked them or not. Vita laughed.

"Girl, just get what you want you are not gonna put a dent in that stash." Lola picked out five pair of shoes. And they headed to clothes. By the time they left the store they had over ten bags a piece. The driver put all of the bags in the trunk. They headed to Wilshire to Agent Provocateur, Lola had picked out so many items before she knew it she had basically purchased one of everything. She looked down at her phone it had changed to West coast time it was already three-thirty.

"I guess I better get headed to dinner."

"That's cool. We can meet up tomorrow for brunch. Discuss how your night went." she replied with a devilish grin.

"Maybe." they both laughed.

"Bitch you gon tell me. Drop me off at Four Seasons, Beverly Wilshire."

"Right Away ma'am."

After dropping off Vita, Lola realized she had no clue where they were staying. She was hoping that the driver knew. As they were driving down the freeway, she realized the locations began to look more fancy and spacious. Sprawling hills and all of the cars were Maserati, Porsche and Lamborghini. They eventually exited off and arrived at a gated community. She looked around at the houses and saw that each driveway held a foreign expensive car. Sprawling driveway, beautifully kept yards with swimming pools attached. They pulled into a gated house with a gold fence and lions sat on the columns greeting you as you drove through the gates. A long driveway which could sit about five cars, with a fountain sitting in the middle. She was impressed. Not bad at all she thought.

The driver parked opening the door, Lola got out looking at the beautiful mansion. She had never seen a house like this in her life. It had white columns which surrounded the entrance and balcony that over looked the front door. As she walked up to the door it opened, and an older Mexican woman appeared.

"Hello... Miss Lolita. I'm Rosa." Lo smiled deciding not to correct her. Mister Uno will meet you in dining area at five"

"Oh okay."

"Let me show you your room."

"Okay." Lola looked up at the wall aquarium. It held sharks and tropical fish. *Is that a fuckin' aquarium in the wall? The fuck?!* She looked at the rolling stairs which were ivory with a gold accent. Where it was just enough, but wasn't too flashy. As they walked the halls she realized this house had over six rooms, and all the doors were closed. At the end of the hallway there was a room with double doors, Rosa opened the doors revealing the master bedroom. It was beautiful. A king sized bed, Versace black and gold set. The room had a panoramic view. Lola was in awe.

"Do you need me to get you anything?"

"No thank you."

"Okay. I will return downstairs, until you need me. Or call on the phone, number three, and I will answer for you."

"Oh, okay. Thank you Rosa." The driver had brought the bags up to the room. Lola thanked him and handed him a tip, which he declined immediately.

"No, can do. I am here for you this week." He responded. Lola placed the money in his pocket. "I demand you take it." He didn't oblige and left the room.

Lola looked around the room. It looked like a Kings palace, everything was of a deep mahogany wood that looked as if it never saw a day of dust. She walked over to the double doors curious to what was on the other side. A Jacuzzi that overlooked a pool below. The Jacuzzi was edgeless, with water spilling like a waterfall into the pool below. There was a recliner of gold with a barrier on each side. She closed the door looking around the room again she realized there was no television. Although there was security cams all over the wall. She walked into the walk in closet which was a room in itself. Center island, different sections filled with designer clothes. There was fifty inch television on the wall. She looked over the items inside the island drawers. Ties, jewelry and watches. She had never imagined Uno to be a connoisseur of suits. But, she also had never imagined he was this rich. Maybe tonight she would definitely ask more questions. She touched his clothes which were neatly placed in different sections, by article of clothing. She felt someone behind her.

"Yuh like?" She jumped startled.

"Oh my god, you scared me!"

Uno smiled back at her. "My bad."

"I thought you weren't going to be here until five."

"Its 4:45."

"Oh. Well, I'm not ready yet. I haven't even showered yet."

"Well, we can arrange that together, if that's what yuh like."

She laughed. "Maybe. But, I'm definitely going to need to ask a few more questions about you my friend."

"No problem. Ask whatever yuh want." He smiled at her as she walked away towards the bathroom. Something about Uno was intriguing and mysterious, so far he had been a complete gentleman. Why was he single? She thought. But she wanted him, she wanted him now.

Lola walked into the spacious bathroom. The floor was covered in gold porcelain tile. His and hers sinks. A shower that looked like a waterfall, completely open the ceiling revealed around showing the sky. Uno came into the bathroom. "Let me show yuh how to turn it on." In seconds water came down from the ceiling, it was so relaxing Lo had never seen anything this beautiful. She turned to kiss Uno. He grabbed her body. They both began to step out of their shoes. He grabbed her chin aggressively kissing her breasts through her shirt. She let out a soft coo. He ripped her shirt off her body as he gently removed her brassiere. She began to feel his manhood throbbing through his pants. "Yuh got a fat pum pum." He ran his finger up and down her clit.

"Mmm..." Replied Lo seductively.

Her panties were soon to the floor. He picked Lo up in the air, her legs wrapped around his neck. His tongue playing in between her walls as the water trickled down her back. Her screams echoed thru the room as he pressed her back up against the wall as his face was soon buried between her thighs. Lo clawed at his back in ecstasy.

Two hours later they were lying in bed. Lola's whole body sore; she could barely move her legs. Uno was lying across her chest, sleeping. She looked down at him, he was so adorable. She loved the aggression he showed in the shower. She attempted to get up. He awoke.

"Where are yuh going?"

"To the Bathroom" Uno moved off of her body to the opposite side of the bed. Lola moved her legs slowly off the bed. She walked slowly to the bathroom. Uno smiled at her naked body. Once done she went over to her suitcase she pulled out a silk robe.

"Why are yuh putting on clothes?"

"Because, I don't want to be walking around naked."

"Maybe I like to see yuh naked." Lola slid the robe over her body tying it closed. She walked over to him on the bed.

"You'll have plenty of time to see that." She kissed his lips.

"I know. I'm gonna have that good shit all the time." He pulled her arm over towards him. He grabbed her face kissing her. He reached over to grab the phone. Lo walked back over to her suitcase. Uno began to speak into the phone. His accent loud and sexy as he ordered food.

"What yuh want to eat?"

"Um… maybe baked chicken."

"Baked chicken and pasta that I like." He hung up the phone.

"You have a chef?"

"Of course. What boss doesn't?" he smiled at her. Lola crawled into the bed beside him.

"So, now would be a good time for my questions."

"Ask away."

"What exactly do you do?"

"I'm a CEO. I own a record label, businesses; such as real estate, restaurants and strip clubs."

"And you're in the game?" said Lo.

"Let's just say I get money."

"What is your name?"

"Jeren Navas. Did I answer all of your questions?"

"One more; why are you single?"

"Because I know what I want, and I *always* get what I want."

"So, what does that mean?" said Lola.

"You stay on my team; everything will be at your feet. Fuck me, everything can be gone. I mean *everything*, yuh understand."

"Yea." Said Lo, half unsure of what he really meant. His tone said serious and she felt a little uncomfortable by it. He kissed her cheek.

"Let's go down to eat." He got out of bed she looked at his dick. Nice. She thought about him and her in the shower. She was definitely gonna stay on his team. After dinner they had sex twice more. Great sex and money at her disposal. She could get used to this.

The Team

Two days later Lo had met up with Vita at a restaurant on Wilshire. When Lo arrived a server took her back to Vita. Vita stood up to hug her. Vita was dressed today in pure rock star attire, denim studded shorts that showed off her ass. A white tank that revealed her stomach and studded Louboutin sneakers. Diamond bamboo earrings glistened in her ears.

"What's up chick!" shouted Vita.

"Hey!" They hugged tightly; Vita let go to look at Lo's outfit. She was wearing a black crop top and skirt, Givenchy heels. Her hair was up in a top knot with back out.

"Look at you diva! Haven't seen you in like two days. What's good?"

Lola laughed shyly. "I've been spending time getting to know Uno. We went shopping and have been sightseeing between his meetings."

"Mmmhmm. Just sightseeing, I bet all up in through your thighs!"

Lo burst into laughter. "What you trying to say?" Lo replied rolling her neck sarcastically.

"Bitch, you smiling ear to ear. You got a new canary diamond bracelet on your wrist. Who do you think you fooling?"

"Well, yes we have slept together. It was fucking amazing! I'm feeling him."

"Well, I'm happy you guys are hitting it off. He's been talking to Mill about you."

"What did he say?" replied Lo excited.

"He was like you're a fly bitch and he like being with you."

"Okay. That's cool."

"I'm really happy for y'all. But tonight were going out to this club with a few of my girls out here."

"Okay. I'm in. What you been up to?"

"Shopping, the other day I was so fucked up I couldn't even get up."

"What!"

"Yea. I had been drinking and shit and fell out in the shower bitch." Lo laughed out loud.

"What did Mill say?"

"That night he was out all night handling business. Fucking housekeeping woke me up." Said Vita as she sipped from her glass.

"Well bitch get that together tonight, I don't want to have to pick you up off the floor."

"Girl, please. You better not come there with any hickies and shit. Yea, you can still see that shit through the makeup."

Lo laughed again. "I thought I covered it good."

"No bitch." They burst into laughter again, Vita always made Lo laugh and their new bond and friendship had become what Lola liked most. She had never had a homegirl. Definitely none like Vita who understood her humor and had her back.

It was after six-thirty when Lo had the driver take her to the house to get dressed. When she arrived at the house she saw Uno's driver was still there. A smile came to her face. The driver opened the door and she hopped out of the car. Rosa met her at the door.

"Hi, Lolita, mister Uno will see you upstairs."

"Okay, thank you." Lola rushed up to the bedroom.

"Uno, said Lo as she took off her shoes as she climbed on top of the bed. Uno stood at the bathroom entrance staring at Lo.

"Hi, babe, how are you?" said Lo.

Uno walked over to the bed.

"So, I'm supposed to eat dinner alone?"

"Huh? What are you saying?" said Lola confused. Uno looked directly in her eyes his face stern.

"Yuh not understanding me now, huh? His accent became piercing. What I tell yuh?"

"Don't talk to me like I'm a kid. A'ight." She shouted defiantly.

"You realize whose fucking house you're in? I say what the fuck I want to say when I want to say it. You're with me! I told yuh we meet breakfast, lunch and dinner! He pointed his finger in her face; unless I say fucking otherwise!" he shouted, his voice sounded as if rang out throughout the house. Lola got off the bed.

"You're not gonna talk to me like this! Over, a fucking dinner? Fuck you!"

He laughed.

"Fuck me? Get the fuck out of my house! He grabbed her by the back of her neck. Fuck me? Take your ass back to fuckin' Atlanta!"

Lo turned around angrily, she slapped his arm.

"Get your hands off me!"

"Get my hand off you? You weren't saying that when yuh were sucking my dick last night. That's what yuh want huh? Yuh want this dick?"

He grabbed her, picking her up and gripping her neck tightly. Lola screamed.

"Get the fuck off of me!"

She began to kick and scream as he carried her into the closet. He grabbed a belt tying her hands up. She kicked him wildly aiming for his face. He pulled out a gun placing it to her neck.

"We can do this my way or your way. But, your way will be your last."

She kicked again. He hit her with the barrel of the gun. She let out a blood curdling scream as blood trickled from her forehead. He ripped her crop top off, and began choking her throat as he kissed her breasts. Lola kicked again; he hit her across the face again. He flipped her over kissing her bare back as he pulled up her skirt and slid his dick inside of her. She squirmed her body from side to side, attempting to fight him off.

"NO!! Fuck you!" she screamed. He began to go deeper. Lola screamed out in pain.

"Fuck me? Huh? Yuh gon' listen next time. What I say goes, yuh fucking understand!"

He continued fucking her roughly as he grabbed her throat again choking her. An hour later, Lola was lying naked covered in blood. Her arms bruised and bruises covered her neck. She couldn't move. Her rectal was sore as well as her vagina. He had fucked her in both holes with the gun, roughly. He stood over her. She quivered, her body weak. He knelt down beside her.

"I'm gonna ask yuh one more time. Are yuh on this team?" Lola's lip was covered in blood. She couldn't get out her words, as it began to quiver.

"Come. Use those pretty fucking lips of yours. What is it?"

He cocked the gun. "Your team." She replied weakly.

"Smart choice. Clean the fuck up. Don't try any shit." He kissed her cheek getting up off the floor. Minutes later he was showered and headed out the door. Lola cried softly to herself.

Three days later they were to be boarding their flight back to Atlanta. Since the incident Lola was in a daze. She feared for her life a feeling she had never felt before. She always felt that she could take on anyone and have no fear. This had changed her psyche and esteem. She hated that she was vulnerable, the incident left her paranoid. The bruises were still visible on her neck but she hadn't left the house since it happened. She thought of going to police, but thought about her possible charges from the car theft. Who would believe her anyway with her priors? So she stayed quiet.

Uno came in the house; she jumped up to meet him at the stairs.

"Hi babe" She kissed his cheek.

"What's up? Get packed up so we can go."

"Okay. I'm ready." Lola wheeled her bag to the door. She was wearing black skinny jeans and a silk button down blouse and studded flats. She placed an oversized pair of Dolce & Gabbana shades over her eyes. She sat at the bottom of the stairs waiting on Uno. Uno soon came down the stairs in a black Gucci V-neck shirt, dark denim jeans and a pair of Jordan sneakers. She was in shock to see him dressed this way, he was normally dressed clean. Lola stood up to follow his lead.

The driver was waiting and in minutes they were on a private plane back to Atlanta. During the flight, he was quiet, texting on his phone or on his MacBook sending messages. He looked over at her.

"We have a dinner party to attend Wednesday night. It's important, I need yuh to get your shit together and be fucking flawless. Understand?" Lola looked in his eyes, thinking in her mind how ironic it was that he wanted her "*flawless*". She had a black eye, swollen lips and bruises on her thighs, but he wanted flawless.

She shook the daydream out of her head as she came back to reality, Uno was in front of her face staring into her eyes.

"Do yuh understand?"

"Yea, its fine" She replied solemnly.

"I got everything set up at the house. Same rules apply."

Lola nodded her head. She looked out the window. Welcome to the team.

* * *

Flawless

The plane landed at Hartsfield International Uno stood up, stretching his arms. As he stretched his arms out, a gun was revealed on his waist He looked over at her.

"I have some business to handle. The car will take yuh to the house. I'm gonna see yuh at dinner."

"Okay." She stood up slowly fixing her blouse. They stepped off the plane and Uno rushed over to a SUV as Lo walked over to a Bentley. The driver stood waiting beside the car. He was a medium build, Trini, late fifties.

"Hi, Miss Lola. Pleased to meet you." He took off his hat, revealing his bald head, as he bowed before her.

"Nice to meet you." She replied with a smile. "My name is Nate, I will be your driver."

"Okay." She replied nervously as he opened the back door for her. She sat down quietly. As they drove home she began to search for her phone. She wondered what Vita was doing and if she had any ill feelings towards her since they hadn't spoken in days. She found her phone and on the screen said Vita. *See you tomorrow morning. Gladys.* Lo was confused. She began to text back and another message came through from Vita. It was an address, *to Glady's Knight Chicken & Waffles, and said 9:30 am.* She texted back stating okay. In moments they approached the house, it was an exact replica of the LA mansion. The only difference was his six cars sitting in the driveway.

Lola was not impressed, as she was before. It was more as if it was to be expected this time around. Nate opened the door, to let her out and she walked in the house. The housekeeper at this home was Hispanic and in her late forties. She said her name was Nora and showed her to their bedroom. As she walked in the room there was shopping bags everywhere. Givenchy, Chanel, Christian Louboutin, Dior and Dolce & Gabbana bags.

She bent down to look inside of them. They were all women's clothes. A smile came to her face as she revealed each item, one by one. She walked into the closet area, which had double doors. She walked around the main entrance seeing all of his ties and jewelry placed in glass countertops. He had rows of shoes and clothes lined every inch of the closet. Furs, suits, tees and jeans. Each column, section filled to capacity, all new with the tags still on them.

There was a second set of doors at the side of the closet. She opened it, it led to another closet, which had over seven racks of clothing in them. Identical to the first closet, glass countertop in center Island, and space everywhere. There was a white ottoman in the center of the room.

"What the hell?" She walked over to the shoes, which lined a complete section. She picked a pair up to see if they fit, her foot, they did. She looked in a few more shoes to look at the size they were all perfect fits. She left out of the closet going to the bathroom. His and hers. There was vases of roses all over the floor, all pink. She smiled walking over to the countertop seeing little blue boxes all over. She opened them one by one. Diamond bracelets, earrings, necklaces and the last box was gold it had a card attached to it. *"Welcome to the team, Ma."*

She opened the box is was a beautiful, black and Ruby diamond ring. It sparkled brightly and had diamonds all the way through. She placed the ring on her finger. She couldn't believe he had done all of this. Maybe he was a good guy he just had a few issues. She looked at the ring on her finger and smiled again. "Welcome to the team." She said softly. She heard a light tap at the door. "Yea"

"Hi, Miss Lola, I've come to remove the bags and flowers for you."

"Okay." Lola took the jewelry to the second closet as Nora came in. Lola began to help her.

"No no no, I will put these away for you. You will not lift a finger."

"But, it's okay. I can help you." Said Lola. Nora smiled at her.

"Those are mister's orders, Miss. I am here for you, whatever you need." Lola could tell the sternness in her voice, so she went to sit on the bed. She looked over to the security cameras that lined the wall. She glanced at the time, it was an hour til' dinner. She better not be late.

The next morning Uno was up at seven. Lola awoke to him speaking into the phone. She sat up in bed and looked over at the time on the wall.

"Babe" She said softly. He came out of the closet.

"Good morning baby." He said with a smile. He walked over to her in the bed in a wife beater and slacks. He reached over and kissed her lips.

"What are you doing?" she said.

"I gotta go to New York, for a business meeting."

"New York?" she replied confused.

"Yea, I'll probably be back, late this evening. Yuh don't have to wait up for dinner."

"Okay."

He kissed her lips again slowly, running his fingers through her tasseled mane.

"I want yuh in the house by nine. Understand?" He replied sternly.

"Yea." She replied softly.

"You can take the driver or the Benz CL550 out there. Okay?" Lola nodded. Don't forget about tomorrow, I need yuh flawless. Understand?"

"I understand." He kissed her one last time before going back into the closet. Lola went back to sleep. An hour and half later she was awoken by her cell. It was Vita. Oh shit! Gladys. She answered the phone.

"Hello"

"Yea Chic, you on your way?"

"Yea, give me about twenty minutes."

"Alright, see you there."

Lola hurried into the shower and after slipped into a pair of jeans, black shirt which was fitted and Givenchy tee. She threw on a pair of black studded Louboutin's, and left her hair out flowing down her back. She looked on the nightstand and saw a few stacks of money. A note attached stated, "Have fun."

She threw the money in her purse and went over to the key ring. There was over fifty keys. A few were Mercedes, she picked the bottom one, hoping it was the one. She hurried downstairs; Nora greeted her at the bottom of the steps.

"Hungry, miss?"

"Um… no, I'm going to head out."

"Okay, what would you like for dinner?"

"I may get some food while out."

"What would you want miss, I have it for you?"

"Um, Steak and potatoes. I have to go, I'll see you later." Lola rushed out the door trying the key. It went to a Black Mercedes, she walked around to the back to make sure it was the 550. It had dark tints and black and pink rims. She thought that was a bit odd, but she got in anyway. The seats inside were pink as well. She looked in the passenger seat there was roses and another card.

"A little whip for the misses" Lola screamed.

"This is MINE!! Is he fucking crazy?" She started the car and the gps came on, "Hello, Lola. Where would you like to go today?" She smiled brightly.

"Gladys knight chicken & waffles." The GPS began the route, as she sped out of the driveway.

When she arrived she parked up front and walked into the restaurant. A woman greeted her and escorted her to the back where Vita was. A bright smile came over Vita's face as she saw Lola.

"Good morning lovely!" said Vita as she stood up to hug Lola.

"Good morning to you to beautiful, as always." Vita was wearing a strapless flowing maxi dress with green and pink flowers all over. She was wearing a pink diamond necklace and her hair was in a long side braid. The braid accented her beautiful bone structure. "I ordered us some uptowns; you have to try this lemonade mix. I fucking love them. Lola laughed at her excitement in the drink. So, what's good? How are you?"

"I'm ok, I guess." said Lola nervously. She pulled her hair out of her face.

"You guess. Hold up, boo! What is that? Lola panicked thinking could she see her bruise that was still slightly visible on her chin. She looked at Vita, pointing at the black diamond ring. He gave you this? Lola put her hand out so she could see it. He really loves you girl. Only the crew can give out the black & red diamonds. I have a bracelet, Mill gave me long time ago, and I wear on occasions."

"What does it mean?"

"Red stands for blood family, Black for the bond." said Vita. If anyone sees this, they know what's up. You with the ring mean you're the first lady.

"I mean, isn't this a little soon? We've just gotten to really know each other." Lola replied.

"Well, that's how niggas do. They lock it down on what they want. Besides I heard that Uno has been talking a lot about you."

"Saying what?"

"Like he's smitten and shit." Said Vita with a smile.

"Everything is happening a bit fast. I want to get my own spot, ya know."

"We can do that today if you want. We can go shopping get our mani and pedi. Shoot maybe a touch up, because my hair feeling dry right now. So are you gonna be living with Uno?"

"I mean, right now, yes. He had roses, diamonds and racks of clothes waiting for me when we arrived yesterday. It was very sweet."

"Wow. Uno is very connected can get you anything you want."

"Yea, he said there's a dinner party tomorrow night, we have to attend."

"Oh, for his label. He's supposedly signed a few new artists. You know that song, Zoned out?"

"No."

"It's by a rapper named Legend. He's about to be signed to Uno's label, Diamond Records. Big on social media and shit."

"Oh, I'm not good with technology. But, I guess I will hear it tomorrow."

"So, we gotta pick you out something fly today."

After they were done eating they walked out to the cars. They decided to ride in one car. So they took Lola's car home. She got into Vita's car.

"Bitch, he got you the 550?"

"Yea, I got that this morning."

"That's what I'm talking about boss bitch. But, I called up a few realtors and got a few places for us to see in Buckhead."

"Okay. Let's go."

They spent the next two hours viewing places. Lola found a condo she immediately fell in love with. Two bedrooms, two bathrooms, exclusive community. She put down the money immediately and the realtor said she could move in by next week. They headed to the mall.

"Girl, your place is gonna be fabulous. We can get some cute things for your living room, that balcony area is nice."

"Yea, I think I'll like it. But, this place is between you and me." Said Lola sternly.

"I got you. You're my girl; whatever goes on is always just between us."

"Okay." Lola smiled.

"Just remember anything you need or you need from me, I got you. You are like the little sister, I never had." Lola laughed. "Appreciate it."

After being at the mall all day, Lola returned home around seven. She walked in the door and was greeted by Nora. "Good evening, Miss. Do you have bags for me to get?" "Um… Nate has them."

"Okay. I have steak, baked potatoes and asparagus prepared for you. Will you have dinner downstairs or upstairs?"

"Um… I will have dinner downstairs in about twenty minutes." Nora bowed her head and retreated back to the kitchen. Lola went upstairs to take a bath. As she lay in the tub she gazed at the ceiling thinking about her nana. She began to wonder if she was okay, had she been eating. She became filled with emotion. After she was done she went to her phone and blocked her number first before calling Nana. The phone rang three times. Lola began to expect the worse.

"Hello. My Lola? Is this you?" said Nana weakly.

"It's me, Nana."

"Oh, praise God. You are okay, my child. I have been worried sick about you."

"I'm fine, Nan. How are you? Are you eating?"

"I'm okay. Angie from the church has been helping me. The police had come by asking about you. Asking me all types of questions."

"Well, don't worry about that. I'm fine and I love you."

"I love you too, baby. So where are you?"

"I gotta go. I love you more than anything. Be sending you something soon."

"Okay. You be safe. Remember, the battle is not yours..."

"It's the Lord's." Lola chimed in. that was one of her Nana's favorite quotes.

"It is indeed. He will never forsake you. He will love you for eternity. You understand?"

"I know. Gotta go. Love you." Lola hung up the phone, a smile spread across her lips. She went downstairs to eat and by nine she was in bed. She felt strange lying in the big empty bed without Uno. She looked to his empty side of the bed, massaging it with her hand. She did miss him a little.

Around one-thirty in the morning she heard Uno come into the room. She heard his bags thud to the floor.

"Baby..." He said as he began to take his clothes off. Lola turned to his side of the bed.

"How was it?"

"Good. We gotta go to Miami, next week."

"What?" said Lola rubbing her eyes.

"I got business to handle. I stay for days, yuh stay for days." He climbed into bed. She moved up to lean on his chest. He kissed her lips. He began to run his fingers through her hair as he kissed her neck passionately.

"I was thinking about yuh the whole flight home."

"Oh yea" She replied seductively.

"Yea, thinking how much I'm gon' tear this pussy up tonight."

He moved down her body pulling her underwear to the side, in her satin camisole. He thrust his fingers inside her sugar walls. She screamed. He smiled at her screams as he climbed on top of her and her mind drifted away.

The next morning Lola awoke to the sound of a kettle, she sat up in bed wiping her eyes. As she focused in on everything she realized, Uno was at the foot of the bed.

"So, It's my job to fucking wake yuh up for breakfast?"

"What? I thought…"

"Shut the fuck up! What did I fucking tell yuh in LA?" His voice began to ring out throughout the house. Lola sat up.

"Look…" she replied defensively.

"Oh, yuh about to say some shit? Yuh don't tell me fucking look, I run this shit!"

He then grabbed her by the foot dragging her to the floor. Her head hit the bottom of the king size bed frame as she kicked him off. One of the kicks hit him in the mouth. His eyes filled with rage as he looked down at her. He then smiled at her.

"Have your ass here at five. So we can be out by fuckin six. Am I clear?"

"Yes"

He got off the floor leaving out the room. Lola sat confused wondering why he didn't strike back, she knew he wanted to. She got up from the floor and walked into closet to pick out her clothes for tonight. As she began to look through her racks of clothes she felt something drip on her back. She went into the bathroom and realized her head was bleeding.

She began looking through the cabinets for alcohol or peroxide. She got on her knees searching in the cabinet below the sinks and found jewelry boxes. She looked inside of one seeing different black & red diamond jewels inside. She pulled one out; it was a woman's ring. It was old a bit flawed. She threw it back in the box; she then saw another jewelry box and inside it was filled with pills. She heard Uno coming up the stairs she grabbed some peroxide and got off the floor. He came into the bathroom.

"I'm getting ready to go. Be here by five." He kissed her cheek. Lola rolled her eyes as he left the room.

Around two in the afternoon, Vita called. Lola asked her to come over and see the outfit she had chosen. Vita told her she would come by to do her makeup and hair as well. Around three, Vita showed up with all her supplies in tow. Nora greeted her at the door, surprised.

"Hi, ma'am, one moment." She walked over to the intercom to tell Lola, Vita was here. Lola came out the room in a spaghetti tank and tights. She smiled at Vita.

"Hey girl! Come upstairs." Vita followed her up the stairs. She came into the foyer area of the bedroom and sat down on the couch.

"This place is gorgeous. The décor is everything."

"You had never been here before?"

"No. I've heard about it. This shit is fuckin' fly the detail put into this shit. So fuckin' bomb!" Lola laughed. She walked into the closet and pulled out a Herve Leger black embroidered fringe gown. "So, this is what I chose. I want you to tell me what you think?"

"Well, put it on so I can get full look at it." "Okay." Lola took off her shirt and tights she realized, she had a minor bruise on her thigh, luckily the dress covered. Vita smiled as Lola turned around. "This is fucking beautiful Lo. Some fly strappy heels and some accessories. Your hair pulled over to the side. Soft curls. Yes!"

"Cool. Let's make me beautiful!" Lola took off the dress and put back on her clothes.

An hour later Lola was dressed and ready to go. She looked flawless, the dress accentuated her every curve, and her makeup stunning. Vita stared at her in admiration, she snapped her fingers.

"Boy, I swear I should get paid for this shit! I'm a beast." Lola looked at herself in the mirror, she smiled brightly.

"Oh my God! Look at me! Thank you so much V!" "Anytime, girl." Lola hugged Vita tightly. She heard a loud voice in the driveway she knew it was Uno. Vita had begun packing up her things. She headed for the door.

"Well, I'm about to go. Have fun and call me tomorrow."

"Of course I will." Said Lola. Uno was now standing in the foyer.

"How you doing, Vita?"

"I'm good." She replied with a smile.

"Tell Mill, I need to speak to him." He replied sternly.

"I'll let him know. Bye Lo"

Vita proceeded downstairs. Uno looked over at Lo, his eyes piercing her. She touched her neck, feeling the tension in the room. He smiled.

"Yuh look beautiful."

"Thank you." He walked over to her. He kissed her cheek gently walking into the closet. Lola let out a sigh of relief.

The music was blaring inside of the venue. It was an A list affair of Atlanta's elite at the party. Everyone was dressed in gowns, red carpet and press everywhere. They were escorted to their table. Uno pulled out her chair, smiling as onlookers stared. When someone shouted out his name, he quickly turned around to speak to an older Italian man with a sexy young blonde on his arm. Lola looked around the room, seeing a who's who in music. She looked to the table beside her and saw Kamai. She was a multiple Grammy winner, beautiful, whose songs were played on every radio station. She was star struck. She looked away towards Uno. He was talking to the Italian man, and a milk chocolate complexion guy. He was sexy, and definitely caught her eye. He was wearing all black, full beard and diamonds glistened from his neck. He smiled and his bottom row of teeth glistened as if diamonds were in them. Lola couldn't turn away. Uno turned around facing Lola.

"Baby, I want you to meet the latest addition to the family." Lola snapped out of her daydream. She looked up to see Uno bringing the eye candy man, to the table.

"Legend meet first lady Lola. Lola my new triple platinum artist, Legend" Lola and Legend made eye contact. She stared into his dark brown almond eyes, he smelled great, handsome and street.

"Pleasure to meet you Miss Lola." He shook her hand. He smiled at her. She smiled back.

Uno was whisked away by a publicist. Legend looked at Lola again.

"So, where are you from First Lady?"

"Florida." She replied softly, keeping her eyes on where Uno was. He was now across the room surrounded by other music execs. She looked up into Legend eyes. He was smiling back at her. She stared at his profound high cheek bones and dimples. "Where are you from?" she said staring into his eyes.

"LA. I'd like to show you around, next time you're on the west coast."

She laughed. "Are you flirting with me Mr. Legend?"

"Nah, just extending an invite to you when you're in my city, hit me up."

He smiled again. She looked over to where Uno once was, he was gone. She frantically looked around for where he could be. She saw him on the stage, he looked in her direction. She quickly sat down at the table. She didn't need any drama tonight. They began to talk about the label's many accomplishments over the year; she stared at Uno's bright smile. How charming he was and how his face lit up as he talked about his many artists. On stage he was a sweetheart. Maybe she had it all wrong, maybe he was just stuck in his ways. Maybe she could change him. She looked across the room seeing Legend, looking at her. She immediately looked away.

They headed home around one. Lo was exhausted, she had danced, taken pictures and was stuffed from all the food everyone she met pushed her to try. As the driver whisked them through downtown Atlanta, Uno was quiet, looking out the window. She placed her hand on his lap.

"I had an amazing time tonight. Thank you for inviting me."

He chuckled. As they pulled up to the house, he stared at her. "Yuh looked really beautiful tonight."

"Thank you." The driver parked the car, and proceeded to open the back door. Lola stepped out adjusting her dress; Uno came behind her, taking her hand. They walked into the house, heading upstairs. Uno walked into the closet; Lola sat on the ottoman taking off her heels.

"So, did yuh think I forgot?" shouted Uno from the closet.

"Forgot what?"

"Yuh know that bullshit yuh pulled earlier, kicking me."

Lola hurriedly tried to take off her other heel. Uno came out the closet, shirtless wearing his boxers, something was in his hand. Lola finally got the heel off.

"Baby, listen." She began to plead. She looked in his hand and realized it was a whip clutched in his palm.

"Why are yuh like a fucking child, I gotta fucking beat every day!" He moved closer towards her.

"Uno…" He swung the whip hitting her across her bare back. She screamed out in pain as she fell to the ground. He grabbed her by her hair, "and don't have that bitch in my fuckin' house ever again! The fuck wrong with yuh! He punched her in the face. This is my fucking house!" Lola tried to shield herself, as he kicked her in the chest.

"How the fuck does that feel? Huh!" he screamed as he kicked her repeatedly. Lola couldn't scream anymore. He pulled out the whip and began beating her again. She laid in the fetal position as her body grew numb.

The next morning, Lola woke up on the floor. Her dress ripped and her body ached. She couldn't move her legs. She tried to put her hands out to reach for her phone. She couldn't find it. She screamed for Nora.

In minutes she arrived. A look of horror came across her face as she approached Lola.

"Oh my, miss. You okay?"

"I can't move my body. Can you please run me some bath water, and help me into the tub?"

"Certainly, miss. She began to run the water. You want me to call a nurse?"

"No, please, don't." said Lola frightened by the thought of being whipped again. Nora went into the closet getting a chair to place Lola on in bathroom so she could remove her clothes. Lola glimpsed at herself in the mirror. Her lip was busted and bloodied, her eye half shut, whelp marks all over her body. She began to cry hysterically. Nora hugged her, helping her into the bathtub.

D4L

Lola stayed inside for two weeks. The trip to Miami had been postponed. The second week when she fully regained her strength she decided to return Vita's calls. She told her to meet her at the signing of her condo. She was to get her keys today, and she had furniture coming. Lola wore dark oversized black shades, black thermal top and jeans. Her hair was dry and in a tasseled bun. Vita was running late and Lola had already gotten her keys and was inside waiting on Vita. She heard the clicking of heels on the marble floors outside she knew it was her. There was three loud knocks at the door. "Who is it?"

"Who else bitch?!" Lola smiled opening the door. There was Vita flawless like always, wearing a black Moschino dress that stopped at her knees but accentuated every curve. Pink Christian Louboutin heels to match. She hugged Lola tightly.

"How you been stranger?"

"Okay."

Vita closed the door sitting on the island in the center of kitchen. "Now, what's going on? Every other week you buck me for days on end. I'm not stupid, something is up. What's going on?"

Lola clenched her fingers together." I was busy. Uno had a lot going on that I had to be part of." She leaned on the counter beside Vita. Vita reached over pulling her shades from her eyes. She gasped at her semi present, black eye.

"Lo... seriously. He puts his fuckin' hands on you?"

"Vi, don't say shit, okay." Said Lola defensively.

"Lo, you are better than this. Don't stick around, thinking you have to baby girl."

"I just, don't... want this to be an issue, ya know."

Vita shook her head." I never knew his ass beat on fucking women. Ya know, people said he was a fucking freak."

Lola walked towards the window. "He said he doesn't want you at the house ever again."

"Fuck his house. I will piss all over that bitch, and let's see him put a fucking finger on me. He'll get two to the fucking dome. Vi stays strapped, play wit' me if he want to."

Lola smiled at her reply. "You're crazy girl."

"I ain't playing. Shit, need to get you a piece. I have an extra .380. You know how to shoot?"

"You really don't know me huh. Although, right now I really don't know me." said Lola with a half-smile.

"Well, what do I need to know about you, bitch? You holding out?"

"I will in due time. But, I appreciate everything you have done for me. You've been one of the realest bitches I've ever known." said Lola sincerely.

Vita flipped her hair, placing her hand on her hip, sticking out her chest. "What's with this emotional shit? I'm not going nowhere and neither are you."

She hugged Lola tightly. "You my girl, were gonna be down for life!"

Lola smiled.

"No doubt. Vita pulled a bottle of Champagne out the bag, might as well christen this bitch!"

Lola looked around. "Girl, I don't have any glasses yet."

"Well, guess we gotta take it to the head." She popped the cork and poured it in into her mouth. As the champagne began to trickle down her neck, she handed it over to Lo and she proceeded to drink. Within the next hour the movers had come with the furniture. She and Vita sat on her new suede chocolate couches. Exhausted as if they had just finished hard work.

"All you need is to decorate, with my fabulous taste, dahling. She said in her best snooty impression. Lola laughed. Vita went into her purse and pulled out her mint box. I definitely need one of these." She poured a few into her hand. Chasing it with the champagne. She laid back on the couch.

"So, Miami coming up huh? Me and Mill will be going down."

"Oh really?"

"Yea. I told you most of the time he's on the road, Mill is too. But, I only go if it's a place I can do some good shopping. Meaning LA, NY and Miami clubs are bananas! We have to go one of the nights were there."

"I don't know. He might start tripping." said Lola calmly.

"Fuck him. We're going out! You hear me." Vita shouted punching the counter.

"I guess were going out." Said Lo, half seriously. Twenty minutes later Vita was laying on the couch in a daze. Lola had gone to look around the house to see how things would look. It was coming along nice. A king sized pillow top, memory foam bed lay in her bedroom. Mahogany night stands and matching dresser set. If only her Nana could see it. She would be proud. She walked back out to Vita, she had dozed off with her mint box beside her. Lola picked it up, she began to open the box. Vita woke up. "What's up?" Lola handed her the box.

"Nothing, I better head home for dinner."

"Okay. Tomorrow we should go get things for your house. Hell, half of it will be on me."

"Okay, I will be at your place, bright and early." They laughed leaving the apartment.

What Happens In Dade...

A week and a half later, they were heading to Miami. The same usual routine, there was two cars waiting on the tarmac and Lola took a Maserati this time. She was happy to not have a driver as well. She called Vita immediately to find out what terminal she was located. She told her which terminal and she met her out front. This time Vita had her hair flat ironed and was wearing a bikini top and ripped jean shorts where her butt was hanging out and stiletto heels. Lola got out to hug her. She smiled brightly like always.

"You ready for some fucking retail therapy?"

"Hell yea." They got inside the car and headed over to Bal Harbour. After about two hours of shopping and time at the spa. It was almost dinner time. Lo looked at her phone, she had a text from Uno saying that dinner was cancelled and she could stay out. Lola felt like a teenager with an extended curfew. She nearly jumped up. Vita looked at her.

"What's up?"

"Were going out tonight." Said Lola.

"Alright let's do it. Get ready at my suite." On their way to Vita's room they stopped to get bottles of alcohol. Vita said she wanted to switch it up and got bottles of Ciroc Mango. Lola got two bottles of Henny. She was so happy to be free tonight and she was going to live it up. An hour later, Vita was dressed in a black leotard which was sheer and had black crosses covering her breasts and mesh covering her vagina. A pair of matching sheer leggings to match. The illusion looked as if she was naked, and of course she loved it. She turned around looking at her ass in the mirror. "Bitch, I told you I did not come to play with these hoes!" Lola came out the bathroom. Vita smiled. "Werk!!" Lola modeled her outfit for Vita. She was wearing a nude mesh crop top with crystals covering her breasts. Matching mesh skirt with crystal pattern covering her ass and vagina. "Oh, we need a picture of this shit! Shouted Vita. Vita pulled out her selfie stick snapping pictures as well as them snapping pictures of each other. After they were done, they sat in the room taking more shots. Vita went for her purse, she pulled out her little mint box. Lola looked at her. "Vi, what's that?" Vita looked at her confused.

"What?"

"Come on, Vi, we're girls."

"*My I don't give a fuck potion.* You want?"

"What does it do?"

"Gives me the best fucking feeling ever. Vita poured a few in her own hand, you want some?" Lola looked around. "What the hell." She put her hand out and Vita poured some in her hand. "Get ready bitch for the best time of your life." Vita put the pills on her tongue and Lo followed as they chased it with the alcohol. Cloud nine.

They arrived at Liv. Lola couldn't feel her feet. As they were led to a table in VIP, she felt like she was walking on air. She looked over to Vita, who seemed perfectly fine. Vita smiled at her. "You okay, bitch?"

"I love you, Vi." Said Lola with a smile on her face. Vita laughed.

"You are gone baby girl. Just vibe, let this shit take you on this high."

When they arrived at their table, two bottles were sent over. Vita popped open the Dom Perignon. Lola felt good, all of her worries and inhibitions were gone. She stood up from the table and began dancing. "Dance with me, Vi!" Vita smiled at her. As she stood up and began to dance with Lola. She began to grind on Lo, as Lo began to grind slowly on a pole throwing her hand in the air. They soon had an audience. Vita led Lo back to the table. As they sat down another bottle arrived at the table. Vita smirked. "We didn't order this."

"That's a gift from the guys over there at table two. He says, he wants for you two to come over to their table." Lola looked over to the table. Two muscular men waved saluting their drinks in the air. "They're cute! Let's go Vi." Vita looked over trying to check the guys out. Before she could say anything, Lola was halfway to their table. She hopped up following behind her. Lola had made it there, hand on hip smiling ear to ear.

"Hi, thanks for the bottle."

"No problem, beautiful. Have a seat." said the lighter one. Both men were cute. The lighter looked as if he was Hispanic and Black. He had puppy dog hazel eyes, full beard low cut and deep dimples in his cheeks. Lola smiled at him.

"You have to be the sexiest female in here tonight." Vita arrived to the table. The other asked her to sit down with him. Vita looked over to Lola, as in what are we getting into. But, she had her girl's back to the end.

"So, what's your name ma?"

"Lo. And yours?"

"Dion. But people call me, Dash."

"Why is that?"

"I play football, MU."

"What's that?"

He laughed. "That's the university here. But enough, about me I want to get to know you."

"What do you want to know?" said Lola. She then placed her hand on his cheek. "You're really fucking cute."

He smiled. "Appreciate it."

She then kissed his lips. Vita looked over shocked. As Lola and Dion's tongues began to play in each other's mouths. Lola then sat on top of his lap, straddling him. Her dress almost revealing her kitty. She placed her hands on his face kissing him again. He kissed her softly, kissing her cheekbone and chest. Lo giggled as he continued to kiss her softly. She began to grind slowly on him and his manhood began to rise under her as she moved up and down. She smiled feeling his nice sized package beneath her, she wanted more. Vita had begun making chit chat with the guy she was with. She looked over and saw the guy had Lo laid back on the table, with her vagina almost in his face as he began to kiss her bare stomach. He pulled her down to her ear.

"I want you ma." He said in her ear as he kissed her ear. The hotness from his breath began to turn her on. She became warm all over as her sugar walls began to cream in her lace thong.

"Let's go." She whispered. She got off his lap and took his hand leading him away from the table. Vita jumped up from the table, she took Lo's hand, pulling her away.

"Lo, are you really about to do this?"

"I want him, Vi. I'll be good."

"Are you sure?"

"Yes. Just be here when I come back."

"Alright. I'll be here." Vita slid her a condom. Lola took Dion's hand as they left towards the door. "You want to get a room?" Said Dion.

"Of course. They walked a few blocks down and he paid for the room. About an hour and half later she was lying in his arms. He was amazing. Gentle, yet aggressive and the way he threw her body around, she couldn't help but scream out in joy as his ten inches journeyed deeper into her. He looked into her eyes.

"You're one beautiful ass woman. I definitely want to get to know you." She smiled.

"I don't live here, Dash."

"Where do you live? I'll pick whatever team is where you are." He smiled.

"A team?"

"I'm a quarterback. About to go pro soon." She smiled.

"You're just too cute."

"Man, stop with that. I'm just a regular nigga. I want to get to know you, and know everything about you."

"I'm not like these other hoes."

"So, what that mean? I want you."

He kissed her bottom lip gently. He caressed his fingers across her scarred back. She cringed as he continued to kiss her scars. Lola smiled as she relished in the fact for one night, she felt like the most beautiful girl in the world.

The next morning she woke up confused. Her head was spinning. She looked around the room. Realizing she was at Uno's house. She looked at her body she was dressed in a black shirt and cotton shorts. She looked at the clock it said nine-thirty, she got out of bed heading downstairs to breakfast. She didn't remember coming home. She saw Uno at the table.

"Good morning." He said as he sipped coffee.

"Good morning". She replied as she kissed his cheek.

"Yuh have fun last night?" said Uno as he looked at her. Scenes of last night began to play vaguely in her head until she thought about Dion. She remembered herself screaming as he sexed her. She thought of his strong hands caressing her soft ass. She looked at Uno.

"It was okay." She said nonchalant. He looked at her. "When yuh pulled up last night, I said yuh were fucked up. Yuh and Vita had a slumber party?"

"Yea, we went out for a couple drinks. But, we stayed in and got wasted. Didn't want to be out and who knows what happen you know?"

"That's what she said. But, long as yuh safe." They finished eating breakfast and Lola walked upstairs. Minutes later Uno came upstairs stating he was leaving. Lola went to the tub. She looked at her phone flooded with text messages. Majority were from Vita, the others were from Dion.

"I want to see you again."

"Can I see you after practice?"

"Did you get home safe?"

She smiled thinking of Dion. She decided to take a shower and head to Vita's ASAP. Once she arrived at Vita's suite, she was lying in her bed, hung over. Lola came in and lay in bed with her.

"What's up hooker?"

Lola laughed out loud. "I don't remember shit about last night!"

"Yea, 'cause you was fucking gone last night. I didn't know what you were gon' do."

"Yea, so what happened last night? How did I get home?"

"Girl, after you met ole boy, you dipped for about three hours and y'all went to the plaza. Then he said he wanted to take you home, to make sure you were safe, or pay for the cab. I said I would take you. I brought you here gave you a shower and shit. Cause you smelled like sex and fucking Issey Misyake. I had a driver take you home and Mill brought the Maserati by this morning."

"Oh okay. I can't believe I did that last night." Lola shook her head.

"Was it good?"

"Bitch Yass! He was so sweet. He made me feel like the most beautiful girl in the world. Flaws and all, I loved it, it was everything I fucking need right now."

"What about Uno?"

"I mean it was only a one-time thing. What he doesn't know can't hurt him right?" They both laughed.

"So, I'm in for today. Maybe later on tonight we can get some wine?"

"Okay. Hit me up. I'm gonna hit up a few stores."

"Alright, Lo." Lola left, heading to a wireless store. She purchased an LG smartphone and immediately texted Dion. "This is Lo. What's up?"

"Ready to see you. Just tell me where."

Lo smiled. "I'll meet you at the plaza again."

"Alright, see you in fifteen." Lola checked her lip gloss in the mirror as she parked in the parking garage. She exited the vehicle walking to the elevator thinking about Dion. *Who was this sexy, sweet man? Where did he come from?* She got a room under an alias, and paid cash. She texted Dion the room number and he said he would be there in five. Ten minutes later, there was a knock at the door. Lola came running over to the door. In a crop top and skinny jeans. She looked through the peep hole seeing a dozen roses. She opened the door taking the flowers. Dion immediately smiled grabbing her waist, kissing her cheek as they walked in the room.

"Yo, it's good to see you. I thought I wasn't going to see you again." He sat down on the bed. Lola put the flowers on the counter.

"Aww, that's so sweet. I enjoyed last night with you.   I don't make a practice of being a jump off. But, I want to know more about you."

"What do you want to know?"

"Where you from? What do you do? How old are you?"

He laid back on the bed. "Pittsburgh. On a football scholarship. I'm twenty two. You?"

"Jacksonville. I'm just finding myself and what I want to do. 21." He looked into her eyes.

"You got a nigga, don't you?"

"You got a girl?"

"Nah. But, you didn't answer my question."

"Let's just say there's no ring on this fucking finger."

He laughed. "I like that. So where you live now?"

"Atlanta."

"Oh okay, I'm going there in a few weeks to check out next move."

"Okay, You gonna come see me?"

"Of course. My first stop."

He smiled at her. She looked into his hazel eyes. His dark honey skin glistened on his body in his v-neck white tee and True Religion jeans. Lola liked his build, his body was cut in every way. Along with his boyish smile, and personality, she couldn't help but smile when she saw him.

"So you want to go to dinner, so we can finally have a real date."

"Well, I'd rather have a part two, to last night and then dinner."

He smiled. "That would be round three, beautiful. But, I can arrange that." He leaned over pulling her onto him. He kissed her lips. She threw her hands up in ecstasy. An hour later, she laid in Dion's arms. She looked into his eyes, as he slept beside her. His naked sexy body was covered in tattoos all over his stomach and chest. She caressed his chest softly as he slept. Her body craved this man all of the sudden. Could this be something more?

After he awoke, he looked into her eyes. "You ready to go eat baby?" She said.

"Yeah. Let me put some clothes on."

He got out of bed and Lola stared at his sexy naked body. He had an angel on his back, with a verse under it.

"What is that on your back?" He pulled up his pants, turning around to her.

"It's Psalms 1:3. I'm not the most perfect Christian, but I love my God." He said with a bright smile. That touched Lola, she had never met a man, who proudly spoke about his love for God. She knew Nana would love him; she began to feel warm all over. He put on his shirt.

"Are you a Christian?"

"I know his love, but I haven't been the best follower."

She ran her fingers through her hair. "It's all good. Long as you know him, ma. Nobody's perfect, we all got a long way to go." He kissed her cheek. She smiled.

"So, where are we going that has amazing food, that's out of Miami." She said.

"We can go to Coral Springs, Hollywood, wherever you want beautiful."

"You have a car?"

"Of course." She looked at her iPhone, no calls. She turned the phone off and when they went into the garage. She placed it in the Maserati. Dion was a bit ahead of her and didn't see her drop the phone off. When she followed him to his car, he opened the door for her, it was a Dodge Charger, latest model, black on black with dark tinted windows. He made sure she was in safely before he walked around to the driver side. They headed over to the restaurant. Once there, he had valet park the car. Once inside people began to stare at them, and smile in admiration. A little boy came over to him.

"Can I have your autograph?" Dion smiled.

"Sure, little man. He took the pen and paper. What's your name?" "Michael." "Alright, I got you." He signed the paper and gave him dap as he walked away. Lola smiled, watching Dion's interaction with the young boy was sweet. Something about him drew everyone to him. His energy and spirit were magnetic to everyone who came in his presence. They were assigned to a back table.

"And you said you played for Miami?"

"Yea. He chuckled. That's not important right now, I'm trying to learn more about Miss Lo."

"My name is Lauren. My people call me Lola."

"I like that better than Lo."

She smiled. "So, do you have brothers and sisters?"

"Yea. One of each. Brother in the Navy. He's older. My sister, is my twin, she's at Spelman."

"Oh wow, you're a twin."

"Yea. That's my heart there. She not sure what she want to do, but that's alright we got time to figure it out. Ya know. My parents never put too much pressure on us to figure out what we wanted to do. Do what you love and they'll be happy."

"Yea. That's good. So your parents are married?"

"Yea. My mom is from Belize raised in Philly. My dad's family from Egypt, raised in California."

"That explains your beautiful eyes." He smiled.

"What about your family?"

"I don't really know, my parents, except the fact that they are Thai & Trini."

"Sorry, to hear that. So, who raised you? If I may ask?"

"I was adopted, by the most beautiful woman ever."

Dion smiled. "That's all that matters." He reached across the table to kiss her. She kissed him slowly as he held her chin. As they ordered their food, she realized she had fallen for him. She had never told someone so much personal information about herself. She looked at the crease that formed in his mouth as he spoke. She realized when he smiled his eyes became chinky and his perfect white teeth, sparkled. He spoke with respect and adoration for her. She smiled; she could stay in this moment forever.

On the drive back to Miami, she and Dion began to freestyle to songs on the radio. He revealed he could beat box and they started making silly rhymes about each other. They laughed so hard, her stomach began to cramp. He turned the stereo down.

"How long are you going to be in Miami?"

"For a few more days."

"Well, I have a game tomorrow. I would like you to come."

"Okay. I'll be there."

"A'ight, So, when we win tomorrow I can see the most beautiful girl in the world."

She blushed. Every time he gave her a compliment it seemed real and genuine. He touched her leg, as the sun began to set on the ending of another beautiful day.

The next morning Lola woke up seeing Uno staring into her face. "Good morning, beautiful."

"Morning" She replied. He kissed her lips, it felt cold and emotionless.

"Sorry, I've been busy these last days we haven't really had time to each other."

"I understand. You're a busy man." Said Lola.

"So what are your plans today?"

"Um, me and Vita are going to go shopping, eat lunch whatever. What about you?"

"I have a few meetings. But, tonight you and I can have dinner together." Lola cringed. She didn't want to have dinner tonight, she wanted to spend the evening with Dion. Hopefully after his big win, she could give him some great, congratulations sex. She realized she was in a daydream, she focused back in on what Uno was saying. She could tell he was pissed.

"Are yuh fucking listening to me?"

"Yea. It's just that we were going to get facials and then get dinner from this great restaurant she was telling me about. Maybe we can have a big breakfast tomorrow?"

Uno smirked. "So, yuh gonna put me off for that bitch?"

"Why she gotta be all that?"

He slapped her. "Don't raise your fucking voice at me. Lola held her face, praying there was nothing more to come. He got off the bed. Here's some money to cover today, I will let yuh know about dinner. He threw a bag of money at her. Are we clear?"

"Yes."

He left out the room. Lola went to the bathroom to check her face, it wasn't bruised. She texted Vita telling her she was on her way over. She got dressed and hurried out the door. She turned the LG phone on as she sped to Vita's suite. She saw she had five messages from Dion. *Good morning beautiful. I can't wait to see you today!* She responded:

*"Have a good game sexy! See you there! *wink*"* He texted back a smiley face. She finally arrived at the suite she parked the Maserati in the garage and left the iPhone inside. When she came upstairs Vita was dressed sitting at the bar.

"Where are we going now?"

"D, has a game today and we will be in the stands. Vita stood up in her YSL tank and booty shorts, paired with a pair of YSL heels, shades on her face.

"You feeling him huh?"

"It's different Vi. I don't know what I'm feeling right now, but I want more, I want all of it."

Vita smiled. "I think you're falling in love, chica. What are you gonna do?"

"I don't know."

Vita smiled. "Well, let's go cheer your boo on."

Lola laughed. "Were getting a driver to take us there and leave your phone. I have my second phone in case of emergency."

"Okay, let's go." They headed over to the Sun Life stadium. There were fans all outside painted in orange & green. Vita looked at them like they were a bunch of fools. Lola dug in her purse for the passes he gave her. She handed one to Vita as she placed it around her neck. Lola placed her YSL shades on her face. As they made their way to their seats, Vita pulled out her mint box. "You want?"

"Um, only one this time." She gave her one and they knocked it back with a bottled water. When the players made their way to the field, she looked over trying to figure out which one was Dion. Until she heard the crowd erupt in cheer as one player came over towards the bench. He placed his finger up, showing number one. The crowd went bananas. And began chanting, Dion! Dion! She smiled realizing that her guy was who they were chanting for. He had a number four on the back of his jersey. He looked in their direction and smiled. She waved at him. He smiled brightly at her, and then saluted to her. His picture came on the screen. Dion Girgis! Lola was definitely smitten.

62-7. Miami won! Dion came over to the section Lola was in with cameras flashing all around. He jumped on the wall she was behind. She laughed at how spontaneous he was being, she leaned forward winking at him blowing a kiss.

"Meet me outside locker room."

"Okay."

Vita was buzzed. "You gonna be okay? Cause I'm about to leave. I had fun."

"Yea, I'll be okay. Thanks for coming with me." She hugged Vita.

"Call me on your way back to Uno."

"Okay. Love you girl."

"Back at you. Fuck the shit out of his sexy ass today." Lola laughed as they headed downstairs. She waited for Dion, as fans continued to scream as they walked towards the parking lot. Minutes later, Dion appeared wearing a wife beater and Nike sweats he smiled when he saw her.

"Congratulations! She shouted as she hugged him. He hugged her tightly as she kissed his neck. He smelled good, Dove soap and Issey Misyake covered his body.

"My bad I'm not dressed appropriate, or anything."

"You're good. Besides this shows all that I like about you."

He smiled as he bent down to kiss her lips, his five foot ten build towered her body. "So, where you want to go?" He said. "Wherever, you want to go."

"Let's go chill at my place, and I cook you a little something."

"You can cook?"

"Yea, baby. Wait till you see the master at work." She laughed at him flexing his muscles. "Okay. We will see. She stretched out her legs. My feet are killing me."

"Come here. I got you." He bent down for her to get on his back. "You're crazy." "I know you've done something to me." She got on his back as they headed to his car.

When they arrived at his Condo, Lola looked around it was contemporary and swank. She knew it was safe area when she saw a white woman running with her dog. Right off the beach, you could feel the ocean breeze. He reached into the backseat to get his book bag. He led the way to his building. When she walked inside it was clean and smelled of jasmine. There was a wall of accomplishments with all of his trophies. "Make yourself at home." Lola looked at the pictures that sat on the shelf. There was a family picture in the middle. His mother was beautiful, petite, caramel skin and black hair layered around her face. His father was handsome, middle weight, mocha complexion sitting beside his wife with his arm proudly around her. He looked like Dion. With his big eyes and warm smile. A girl was standing in the center, wearing a black tube dress her hair pulled to the side. She had honey skin and hazel eyes and the family smile. Dion was to the left and she assumed his brother to the right in Navy uniform. Looked like one happy family. Something she never had. Dion emerged from the room with new clothes on. A white tee and Nike shorts. He saw her looking at the pictures.

"Saw my family huh?"

"Yea. You have a nice family."

"Appreciate it." Dion headed to the kitchen to begin the meal. As he cooked the food, Lola sat at the bar watching. He turned to her.

"So, how long you been with ole boy?"

Lola nearly fell, she never once thought about Uno while with him. "Not long."

"You love him?"

"No." she said quickly.

"I really like you. I've been thinking a lot about you since we met."

"I have been thinking of you too. But, it's a complicated situation. I like what we have right now, and before you say anything let's just see where this goes."

"A'ight. I understand." He said. She got up from the barstool walking over to him, placing her arms around his body.

"I've never felt like this about anyone D."

She lifted the back of his shirt, kissing his back. "So, do what you feel is right. I'm not going anywhere. But, I can't promise I'll wait forever."

She kissed his back again. She understood what he was saying. He was a sweet, charismatic, fan favorite quarterback, who any girl would probably love to take home to their family, but he wanted her. What would she do? He turned around to face her, she kissed his lips and they soon were sexing on the countertop.

No Love Allowed

Days later, they were on a flight back to Atlanta. She had went out with Dion the night before and they had laid on the beach talking about all of their dreams and goals. He told her about what kind of family he wanted, and how Christmas this year he was going to Pittsburgh. Uno never questioned her during the trip, or had any clue to what was going on. He had so many meetings he rarely spent time with her while there, but back in Atlanta she knew that would change. She decided to make things up with Vita and invite her over to her place for brunch. When she arrived home, she sat across from Uno at the table. Eating her pancakes and omelet, she had few words. Uno looked at her. "What's up? How you feeling?"

"I'm okay. Had a little headache, jet lag."

"Make sure you're not fucking pregnant or some shit. I don't have time for that right now."

She rolled her eyes, looking back down at her plate. "I'm not pregnant."

"Good."

She got up from the table. *"Like I want to have a fucking baby with you."* She mumbled as she went upstairs.

"Yuh have something to say?" shouted Uno from the table.

"No." She went into the bathroom and ran the water to take a shower. She stripped her clothes off, thinking of Dion kissing her neck under the water. She smiled as she let the water fall over her body. As she closed her eyes imagining his arms around her, she felt someone staring at her. She opened her eyes seeing, Uno standing beside the shower, staring at her body with a perverted grin. She continued to shower ignoring his stares.

"Dance for me baby." She looked at him as he held himself. She began to dance under the water letting the suds trickle down her body. He came into the shower, fully dressed. He pinned her against the wall, kissing her lips passionately. She turned her head away. He soon revealed himself to her, he grabbed her face.

"Yuh don't want my baby huh?" He laughed. He pushed her up against the wall again, slapping her face. He picked her up and began to thrust his penis inside her. She began to scream. She dug her nails into his neck. He slapped her across the face again. This time she could feel her face swelling. He bent her over and began to pull her hair as he fucked her from behind. He began to shout out in ecstasy. She felt disgusted. After she knew he was trying to cum inside of her, she began to fight; his semen went shooting out of his penis. He tried to jam it back inside of her. He grabbed her throat choking her. She clawed him across the face. His eyes became red. He threw her out of the shower unto the floor. She scrambled to get her robe, as he came after her. He grabbed the back of her robe, pulling her down. She kicked him in the balls. Uno fell back clutching himself in pain. She ran out towards the room door. The door was locked. She went towards the balcony doors, locked. She looked back at the bathroom door and saw Uno standing with a remote in his hand, with a mischievous grin across his face. Lo fell to her feet.

"Yea, what yuh better do."

An hour later, she was beaten and bruised again. She was wedged between the nightstand and bed. She couldn't move, bloody and sore all over, her eyes seemed as if they had red film over them. Lola wiped her eye seeing blood on her hand. She attempted to turn over and saw a bible had fell in the midst of the attack. She turned the bible to Psalms 1:3.

"And he shall be like a tree planted by the rivers of water, that bringeth forth his fruit in his season; his leaf shall not wither; and whatsoever he doeth shall prosper."

She began to cry loudly. It took her a week to recover this time. That next Wednesday she took a driver, to her place. Vita was to meet her there. She called Dion while she was halfway there. They hadn't talked since she arrived back to Atlanta. He answered on the first ring.

"What up sexy." He said happily.

"Hi, baby. How are you?"

"I'm good. But, what's been up with you I've been calling you almost every day. Worried sick about you! I'm coming to Atlanta on Friday. So I was going to look for you, if you hadn't answered." She smiled at how sweet it was that he was so concerned about her.

"I'm okay. Just had a few things come up. I'm really sorry. I miss you."

"Yea, I miss you too. Grew on me. Will I be able to see you Friday?"

Lola became so excited. "Of course. I can't wait to see you!"

"Yea, my flight get in around noon. Can you pick me up from airport?"

"Of course. Um, where are you staying? You can stay at my place."

"Um, I was supposed to stay at the Hilton. But, I definitely rather be with you, instead of a room."

"Okay. It's set. You will stay here with me."

"Cool. So how my baby doing?"

"I've been better, I won't complain. I just need a getaway, just get away from everything."

"Where do you want to go?"

"I don't know. Just somewhere no one will know for about a week."

"Let's go on a cruise baby. June is coming and I'll be on a break. We can go to Jamaica or even Bahamas."

"Really? I don't know after all those storms went thru there."

"That's true. Wherever you want to go, I'll make it happen."

"You are so amazing. I love how you make everything so simple."

"I'm just saying, I only want you to be happy, and like you told me, I've never felt like this about any other woman. I always want you to smile. She smiled. But, I gotta get ready for weights. I will see you Friday."

"Okay, I can't wait to see you Dash."

"Give me a kiss."

She laughed. Kissing into the receiver.

"Sound nice and wet. Just like I like my baby." She blushed.

"So nasty"

"You like it. So, I will talk to you tonight."

"Okay. Have fun in the gym. Bye."

"Bye." She pulled up to her condo seeing Vita's BMW. She looked up a rental service on her phone and reserved a Mercedes for next week, with dark tinted windows. She didn't know what she was going to tell Uno, but she didn't care. She smiled from ear to ear all the way up to her condo. Vita was waiting by the door.

"Damn! What happened?"

"I was on the phone with D." She smiled. She opened the door and Vita rushed to the sofas.

"So, what's going on with you? Another week no Lo."

"Vi, when I go missing like that, it's because he put his hands on me and beat me unconscious again."

"WHAT?" screamed Vita.

"Yea. He beats my ass. About anything, doesn't matter. I'm getting tired of it. I just don't know what to do?"

"I can't believe he beats you unconscious. Baby, I will go over there and blow his fucking brains out."

"Vi, he is not worth that. I think now, I just want to go. I'm done with this. His money means shit! He go his way and I go mine."

Vi sat up in the seat. "One thing about that nigga, the way he's been talking about you. He's not going to just let you go."

"What do you mean?"

"He, really likes you. Mill told me he was thinking about taking you to Italy for a vacation. Nigga is sprung."

"I don't want to go anywhere with him. Sometimes the thought of him touching me makes my skin crawl."

"Well, if there is no love there anymore, milk that nigga for every dime he got. I would take all the jewelry he got in that bitch. Everything. You wanna fuck me over; I will fuck your fucking life up royally."

Vita stood up. Lola took off her shades her bruises were still visible. Vita looked into her face. She felt sorry for her bestie. "So, D is coming down next week. I don't know what I'm going to tell Uno, I really don't care."

"You playing with fire having him in Atlanta where, Uno runs everything. But, I like that shit." Lola smiled. So we need to go to spa and hair today."

"That's cool."

"How's Mill doing? I'm sorry I never ask about him."

"It's okay. Oh yea, matter of fact they are going to Chicago this week for business."

"That's perfect."

Friday arrived and Lola was happy. Uno had left for Chicago that morning and she had packed up her clothes the day before to spend the week with Dion. She decided that she was going to leave the cellphone at home. She carried her prepaid phone. She had the driver take her to the mall. Where she had her rental parked, once out of sight she hopped into the car. Speeding to the airport, feeling high on life.

She looked at herself in the mirror. She was flawless. Her hair was layered in long luscious curls going down her back, she was wearing a black strapless dress with Moschino belt and Giuseppe spiked heels to match. A text came through of what terminal he was in, she was so excited she could barely stop smiling. She pulled up to the terminal, seeing Dion standing outside wearing a YSL black shirt , jeans and all black J's. She put the car in park, he looked in her direction. She hopped out the car running towards him. "Babe!"

He dropped his luggage, opening his arms to hug her. He hugged her tightly as she wrapped her legs tightly around his body. He kissed her lips as everyone around watched as he held her in the air, holding her ass in his hands. "I'm so happy to see you." She smiled getting down off of him.

"I'm happy to see you too. Looking sexy as fuck, like always." He smiled. "You need help?" said Lola.

"All I need is for you to do is open the trunk, baby." She opened the trunk and he placed his bags in the back. Lola walked around to the driver side of the car. He soon came and got in the passenger.

"So, how are you D? How's football going?"

"It' going good, thinking I may be leaving soon going pro."

"Really, that's huge. Congrats!"

"Yea, I'm just weighing out my options." Said Dion as he took off his shades. He looked over at Lola, he touched her hair. "Your hair looks really good. I like it."

"Aw, thank you." He kissed her neck. They arrived at the condo, as she tried to help him with bags. He told her he had it. So she led the way to the apartment which she had covered in roses and candles. Dion smiled looking at all the effort she put into the room. "Welcome to my home." She replied shyly. He smiled at her. "Appreciate it." he walked over to her kissing her lips.

"I missed you so much."

They continued to kiss passionately as he picked her up in the air. She let out a moan as he kissed her vagina through her thong. He carried her into the bedroom. He gently pulled down her top revealing her breasts; inching down her clothes. Lola placed her hands above her head as he kissed down low, and in between. He began to bend her legs over her head as he went deeper. She screamed out, grabbing his head. He looked up smiling at her. She looked down at him.

"I love you, Dion. I fucking love you!" she screamed. Hours later they were laying naked in each other's embrace. She began to play with his hands, intertwining his in hers.

"Lola, I'm really feeling you. I know I said I wouldn't wait forever, but, I want you to be near me. Want to lock this in. Just me and you." Lola looked into his eyes.

"You want me to move to Miami?"

"Yea, I want to see you every day. Go to sleep with you at night" She looked in his eyes.

"I need to clear up some last things, but, I promise, I will come where you are."

"A'ight, now you promise. You have to keep it."

"I will." She kissed his lips. She turned the television on as they cuddled for the next few hours.

The next morning Dion went to a few meetings to discuss his plans with possible agents. He told Lola he would return in a few hours. She had gotten up that morning and made him breakfast, and now she was looking through her closet to find the perfect outfit for later, she walked over to the balcony in a bra and Dion's shorts. That afternoon Dion came back from meetings he looked amazing. He was wearing a light blue linen button down Tom Ford shirt and white pants that fitted nicely and pair of Tom Ford loafers. Topped off with a pair of black aviator shades. Lola smiled sitting on his lap. "So, how did it go?"

"It went good. It most likely will definitely be happening for me sooner than later."

Lola kissed him. "Congratulations! I'm very happy for you. Having your dreams come true. I know your family will   be   so   happy!" "Yea. He smiled. I've always told my dad I was going to go pro. I gotta call them later. But, where we going, the aquarium and six flags right?"

"Six Flags? Really?"

"Yea. Let's go have fun."

"Okay. Guess I won't put on any heels." She kissed him changing into jeans and a Givenchy black tee. Black Jordan Heiress sneakers and Black Raybans, made the perfect outfit. When she walked out the room he had his iPhone pointed at her to take a picture. She laughed. "I bet it's a horrible picture." Let's take a better one. He pulled her close to him and kissed her cheek as she gave duck lips to the camera. They snapped a few more selfies before walking out the door. She let him drive her in the rental. That day while they were out, nothing else mattered. She at times didn't care about being discreet, she was all over him and vice versa while in public. Dion gifted her an expensive camera to take in their day. Lola didn't care if anyone began to see, she had fallen in love with this man.

Two days later Lola and Dion had been almost everywhere in Atlanta. She was to host dinner tonight and invited Vita over. Dion invited his sister, who was bringing a friend. Lola was anxious and nervous praying everything went perfect tonight. Vita arrived while Dion was in the shower. She perched herself on the counter toying with fruit in a bowl.

"So, miss wifey how you doing?"

"Okay. I'm a little nervous to meet his sister. I want to make a good impression ya know." Lola checked her lasagna that was baking in the oven.

"You will be good. She will fuckin' love you, and if she don't eh, who gives a fuck." Lola laughed.

"I love you Vi. She chuckled. How you been?"

"Girl, alright. Some things went down in Chicago, you know, your other life, but we will talk about that later."

"Anything serious?"

"Talk later."

Thirty minutes later, there was a knock at the door. Lola was in the room putting finishing touches to her outfit. Vita and Dion were in the living room chatting it up. He walked over to open the door. He opened the door widely revealing his gorgeous twin.

"What's up Bubby!" A name she called him as a kid. He smiled hugging her. Vita stood up, never one to hold her tongue wanted to get a view of his sister. Vita looked her up and down. She was wearing a Yeezus tee and ripped jeans with matching spiked stiletto heels. She was gorgeous, slim thick, piercing hazel slanted eyes with long black hair. She glanced over to Vita. "Hi, I'm Destiny." She extended her hand.

"Dez, this is Lauren's home girl Vita." Vita looked at her stiletto nails and now realized one side of her head was shaved. That took Vita by surprise, she quickly side eyed her discovery.

"I thought you were gonna be this little bougie chick, from what Dion said about you and you a little bad ass."

Destiny laughed. "I like you already. You are beat hunty. Love the Giuseppe's." Vita smiled, hugging her briefly.

"And what are you going to school for, I gotta know." Said Vita bluntly.

"Pediatrician."

Vita choked. "What?! Well turn around let me look at you." Destiny twirled showing off her peach shaped derriere.

"I like you too bitch. You bad."

There was another knock at the door. Lola walked out of the bedroom. Vita reached for her gun in her purse. Destiny smiled opening the door.

"Dion, I want you to meet my boyfriend, Mike."

Vita looked over seeing a medium build guy, wearing a black tee, dark jeans with Gucci belt, and Timbs on his feet. He was wearing a Braves hat and Jesus piece hung from the chain on his neck. He looked familiar she couldn't place where she knew him. He smiled removing his hat, she then realized who he was, Ant's younger brother. Ant was one of Uno's head men. Dion looked him over before shaking his hand. Lola walked over to the stove looking like a doting wife. Decked in a Phillip Lim lace embroidered body con dress, her hair sleek, yet pulled behind one of her ears. Vita defenses immediately went up. She walked over to him.

"And who is this?" she replied defensively.

"This is my boyfriend, Mike, he's a Songwriter for..."

"Boyfriend? Are you sure sweetheart? Because, I've seen Magic Mike, at Lenox square shopping with Kimya."

Mike immediately grilled Vita. Vita then pulled out her phone dialing Lola's phone. Lola walked over to the room to get it. "You got me confused with someone else." Said Mike defensively.

"No, you drive a Black Lexus, blacked out with rims right?" Destiny cringed folding her arms across her chest.

"Umm... yea. But I don't know no bitch named Kimya."

"Don't lie, playboy. This my homeboy sister you playing with. You had a party the other day in Buckhead after party was at Magic City. You know what you did in VIP. She told me."

Mike soon became speechless, how did she know all this information. Destiny raised her hand and slapped Mike across the face. The force was so hard he staggered backwards.

"You fucking bastard! Get the fuck outta here!"

Dion grabbed his sister. "It's time for you to leave, son." Said Dion calmly, but you could hear the tension rising in his voice. Mike turned to leave.

"Fuck you! Screamed Destiny. How could you do this to me?" She grabbed him by his shirt and began to punch him repeatedly. Dion grabbed Destiny again as she cried in his arms, Mike turned around with a look of desperation on his face.

"Get the fuck out!" said Dion. This time his voice was stern and his fist balled up. Mike headed towards the door. Vita walked Destiny over to the couch. Mike walked out the door and Dion followed him outside. Mike massaged his chin as he shook his head walking down the hall. He felt an arm around his neck and a fist coming toward his face. Dion picked him up, by his throat his five foot seven, one sixty, stature dangling in the air.

"Stay the fuck away from Dez. I don't wanna hear or see your bitch ass again. You hear me?" He tightened the grip he had on his neck. Mike shook his head frantically. Dion then tossed him like a ragdoll down the hall.

Back inside Vita was consoling Destiny. "I just want to go home." Said Destiny repeatedly. Dion came back inside after he made sure Mike was gone. After Destiny told him she wanted to go home, he told her he would take her home to make sure she arrived safe. After they were gone, Lola came out the room. "What was that about? Why you called my phone?"

"I just saved your ass a beat down."

"What you mean?"

"That nigga is Los' brother, Uno's right hand man."

"What?! For real?" said Lola panicked.

"Yea. So before you brought your ass out here trying to break bread with his punk ass I had to dead that."

"So that story was for real?"

"Nah. But his fuck ass didn't deny it." said Vita chuckling as she placed her glass up to her lips. So, she didn't need his tired ass anyway, with those ashy ass knuckles and that fake shit on his neck." Lola laughed.

"Thank you. I fucking owe you."

"It's all good. You're my girl, I've got your back always." Lola hugged her. Once again Vita saved the day.

* * *

Fire to the Rain

By Wednesday, Lola decided to go home, to show her face. She decided in her mind, that Dion was who she wanted to be with. The next thing was how she was going to get out. If Uno was anything like Vita said, he would probably beat her to stay. So she had to decide how she was going to get away and it would have to be fast. Dion was back at the apartment, sleeping so she figured she had plenty of time. She had a car service pick her up from the mall. As she approached the house, she realized there were cars in the driveway. She became nervous. She stepped out of the car walking slowly to the door. Nora greeted her at the door.

"Hi, miss Lolita."

"Hi."

"Um, Mister Uno has called and told me to tell you to call him."

"I don't have a phone, mine is lost."

"Umm, he has some things arranged for you upstairs."

"Okay. Thank you."

Lola walked upstairs to the bedroom and saw bags of clothes along the floor. She saw a new Apple box on top of the bed; she knew it was a new phone. She rolled her eyes going to the closet. She pulled down a duffel bag and began to toss things inside before heading towards the door. She began to turn the knob frantically. The door was locked.

"What the fuck!"

She heard Nora's voice.

"I'm sorry miss, he had the door wired for you stay in here until he returns."

"WHAT!"

"I'm sorry." Lola became furious. She walked over to the balcony doors locked. She turned the knob frantically again. She walked into the closet she saw all of his, expensive watches in the center island cabinets. She broke open the glass taking the watches, and placing them in a bag. She thought about what Vita said, she decided to clean him out. She began to rummage through his things finding a stash of guns, and money he had stored in a safe. Being her past life, this was simple to her to break his codes. She pulled down boxes in the closet finding stacks of money, she begin to throw it in a duffel bag. The more she began to think of being locked in a room, rage bubbled inside her.

She cleared out every piece of jewelry and thing of value in the bedroom. She shot the door handle off the balcony door, she threw the bags over the balcony. A smiled formed across her lips as she walked back towards the bathroom.

The next morning Lola awoke to a beautiful Miami sunrise, she pulled back the sheet, letting the sun dance over her naked torso. They had packed up the rental and were on the road. They had drove all night and arrived just before dawn. She ran her hand over the empty spot where Dion had once been kissing her neck, before leaving for training. Lola's phone beeped on the nightstand showing she had a text.

"I TAUGHT YOU WELL BITCH! LOL" Lola smiled looking at the attachment, it was a news report.

"In Buckhead, Atlanta last night Diamond Records, music executive, Jeren Navas home was involved in a horrible fire. The 50,000 sq. ft. mansion was found burned to the ground around nine last night, after neighbors heard a blast. One person was found dead, so far authorities are ruling out arson, and citing the fire may have started from electrical problems. Back to you Tracy."

Lola smiled, happy to have the house and man that she felt had become evil, out of her life. She texted Vita back.

"I'll give you my new info as soon as I get it. Love you forever girl." Vita texted back.

"Got you."

Golden

Two months later. Lola had settled into Miami life quickly. She had become a socialite, and attentive girlfriend. She spent her time at the beach, shopping and cooking. She had bought herself a BMW in cash, with the money she had taken from Uno. Lola had initially planned to get her own place, but with Dion's schedule and latest news she decided it may be best to stay with him. She and Dion were in love and although it happened quickly, he had become the best man she knew. Lola was at home today waiting on Dion, so they could go to lunch. She heard Dion's key jingle outside, she perked up like a happy child.

"Baby, where you at?" He yelled from the door as he slipped off his shoes.

"In here." She said softly from the living room. Dion walked over kissing her lips passionately.

"How you doing?"

"I'm okay. How was training?"

"Tired. I've been really working on my cardio, ya know since draft is coming up. Gotta be right."

"You will do fine, baby." She kissed his lips again.

"Thank you, baby. Let me shower."

"Okay."

She knew he was going to take a shower he always did, before they went anywhere after training or practice. She stood up from the couch, taking off her shirt. She heard Dion shout from the bathroom. She began to laugh.

"Yoooo! Are you serious?" said Dion as he came into the living room holding papers in his hand.

"So, how do you feel?"

"A baby! I'm happy, fuckin' speechless... I don't know what to say." He touched Lola's stomach.

"When did you find this out?"

"I found out Friday. Remember, I told you I kept feeling dizzy in the morning. I couldn't figure out why. I went to the doctor and it's early but I'm pregnant. I never saw myself as a mom. What are we going to do? I mean, how do you feel honestly?"

Dion looked into her eyes. "I'm happy Lauren. I love you, and being with you. A child is a blessing ya know. We are going to be together and wherever my career takes me you two will by my side."

"You love me, baby?"

"You know I love you."

He kissed her lips again. "I've loved you since the day I met you." Said Lola as she kissed him.

"We have to celebrate!" said Dion as he picked her up.

Three months later. Lola's belly began to show and she was eating everything. Dion had become supportive of her with cravings and they had talked to his parents and were to meet at the Draft this weekend in New York. Lola had purchased another iPhone, and hadn't talked to Vita in a week. She texted her to see if she was still going to meet her in New York. Her hair was now black and long. Her face had filled out and her breast would spill out of any top. Dion loved her new pregnant body, he said the weight made her more exotic, and her ass was huge. Her phone vibrated, the message said:

Bitch, hell yea, I will be there. We have a lot to catch up on.

Lola continued packing their clothes waiting on Dion. When he arrived they headed to the airport. New York, NY.

Once in New York, Dion had a driver pick them up from the airport. She felt Dion's hands rest on her stomach. She placed her hands over his as they looked out the window. Dion's new agent Lance Cerelli had made sure they received great reservations at The Four Seasons. Lola was happy to be able to see Vita, take a nap and get some New York food. Once they were settled in their suite, Dion had to leave to do a few interviews and appearances. Lola told him she could go if he wanted. He insisted she get rest, and that he was fine. So she stayed in the room, stating she would check on Vita. He kissed her cheek and headed out the door. Moments later her phone beeped with a message from Vita, stating that she had just touched down and wanted to see her. She messaged the hotel details.

Lola stepped into the shower to wipe away the jet lag and to get herself fly for her bestie. Because she knew if she wasn't Vita was going to rip her a new one. She could hear her saying,

"Pregnant or not, you can't be walking around looking like some bum bitch." She chuckled to herself as she lathered soap onto washcloth.

Over an hour later she was dressed and was fixing her hair, when Vita messaged she was on her way up. Lola jumped up from the couch checking herself one last time in the mirror. She was wearing a bomber jacket and slip dress. She threw on a pair of Givenchy slides. Moments later she heard a rapid knock at the door. She walked over to the door, adjusting her dress. "Who is it?" said Lola.

"Who else bitch?" she heard Vita yell from the other side of the door. She looked through the peep hole and saw her backside, she opened the door. Vita turned to face her.

"What's good bitch!" she screamed. Lola smiled hugging her. Vita placed her arms tightly around Lola as she reached around her basketball belly which stood between them. They walked into the suite. Lola looked at Vita. She looked so different, she had lost weight in her face and body. She was still dressed to the nines, but Vita knew something was up. Vita touched her stomach.

"Oh my God, I can't believe you're pregnant. Look at you!" she shouted excitedly.

"I know. Who would've ever thought? I would be a mother? Damn sure not me." They both laughed.

They walked over to the couches. Vita continued to smile at Lola in admiration.

"So, what's going on Vi?" said Lo, caressing her hand over her stomach.

"Girl, so much. I needed to talk to you in person."

"Yea. I can see it all in your face."

"Seriously?"

"Yea"

"Well... after you went all *Left Eye* on Uno's crib. He's been on a warpath."

"Figured that" Said Lola nonchalant.

"Yea, he was cool in the beginning you know, until the smoke cleared and he realized the housekeeper was dead and it wasn't you. So, he calls me up asking me where are you? And I'm like I don't know where you were, last time I spoke to you, you were going home. So, then I threw in some slick shit about me and you falling out because you owed me money. You know this bastard went off on me and was like why would you need my money this and that, and that he pays my fucking mortgage. So, girl I flipped. Next, he confronted Mill about me saying he needs to get me in check this and that. Mill is heated. It got crazy! So, Uno is staying in one of his smaller houses until he gets another built. But, he called me again yesterday and was like he's going to body me and all this shit."

"Wow! What did Mill say?"

"Girl, Mill is mad at me now. He says just tell Uno where you are and me hiding you from Uno is messing with his money."

"Typical nigga."

"Yea, I know right. So, why I think Uno got people following me?"

"What! Don't tell me they followed you here?"

"Nah. I didn't even fly out of the A. but, lately I've been seeing a black suburban following me through the city. I'm not running from him. You know I stay strapped." Vita laughed.

"So what about you and Mill? I don't want y'all to break up or me be the cause any ill feelings in y'all relationship."

"Girl, I don't know. I've been out so much in the streets lately I haven't even seen him. Ever since he said I should give you up, I've been a little hesitant about his intentions. I don't feel comfortable around him anymore. I mean what if he tries to set me up or some shit for him."

"You think he would do that?"

"Lo, come on! I'm not trying to be naïve here. I don't trust his ass!"

"I feel you. So, what are you going to do? I don't want you living like this because of me."

"Well, I've been on the low for real. Thinking of moving away, I just don't know. Starting over, I hate that shit, ya know."

"Yea. But maybe you can move wherever I am and it can be like old times."

"We'll see. But enough about Uno, how's Dion?"

"Oh he's good. He went to do some appearances. He's excited about the baby."

"Aww. I'm so happy for you, you have your fairytale."

"I know. I'm waiting for the dream to be over. You know how it is, when things are too good to be true it probably is."

They both nodded their head they knew how true that statement was. Lola decided she wanted some pizza. They walked to a pizza shop on the corner. Lola had ate nearly the whole pizza. Vita laughed watching Lola scarf down the last piece. They got into heavy conversation about what Lola's plans were for the baby and what sex she wanted. She told her she didn't really care either way, god willing it to be healthy and give it the stability that Nana strived to give her. Vita was happy for her bestie. "I am going to be the godmother right?" "Of course. You're my sister." Vita smiled that was all the confirmation she needed.

They stayed out until around eleven-thirty, after retail therapy Vita went to her room and Lola took a car service back to their suite. Her phone chimed with a message from Dion. "Where are you baby?" As she treaded closer to the entrance, she felt she was being followed. She turned around quickly, no one was behind her. Lola's heart was racing she placed her hand across her chest.

"Lauren, where you going?" She didn't even need to look, she knew it was Dion, he was the only one to ever call her Lauren.

She smiled turning around. He placed his arms around her body. She kissed him over her shoulder. "What are you doing out here?"

"Was gonna walk down the block and get me a pizza." She turned around to face him her arms wrapped gently around his neck.

"No you're not. Not my future star. Let's get some room service, and I give you a little service instead." She kissed his lips gently.

"I'm down with that." He followed her inside and they went upstairs to make passionate love. The next morning Lola woke up to a room full of voices. She could hear Dion laughing and hear a few male voices. She crawled out of bed feeling a bit sore, but she wasn't going to let anything get her down, it was her man's big day. She walked into the bathroom naked to shower. As she was massaging her stomach with soap, she felt the baby move. She stopped and looked down at her stomach. It was the best feeling, she smiled tears of joy forming in her eyes.

"Mommy loves you already cutie. Your daddy and I can't wait to see you!" She massaged her belly again as the water trickled over her body, she thought about Nana. She wanted to see her so bad, maybe once they were settled she could move her to their location. She heard the bathroom door open. She turned the water off and began to step out. She saw Dion standing in front of her in a white tee and sweats. She smiled

"Today, is your big day baby! Are you excited?"

"I'm alight. I mean, I am happy. But, it's about you and my baby. Securing a future for all of us."

"Aw, you don't have to worry about us. I know you will make sure were set, but I can help out."

"Nope. Your job is to be beautiful." He kissed her forehead. She kissed his lips. "So, who's out there?"

"The fam. They can't wait to meet you."

"Serious? Let me get dressed. I don't wanna keep them waiting." Lola slipped into a white tunic, with distressed jeans. She threw on a pair of thong sandals and she ran a brush thru her hair. Dion had left back out to his parents, she opened the door walking out to them. "Hi." Said Lola shyly. "Hi!" said his mother. She walked over to Lola touching her stomach. Her presence warm yet gracious. Flawless, natural beauty. She was wearing a turtleneck dress which accentuates her curvaceous figure, she was five foot five, hazel eyes and manicured nails. "I'm so happy to finally meet you. I've heard so much about you!" She hugged her tightly.

"I'm Julia and this is my husband David, and our son Paul."

"It's a pleasure to finally meet all of you. Dion has told me so much about all of you." David walked over to hug her, and Paul followed suit. Paul was a lot more handsome then the picture, muscular build, stern eyes and was a good mixture of both parents. He had a strong grip and nice smile with a small gap, which showed with deep dimples.

"I've already claimed my nephew. Just gonna put it out there Paul, is a good name. I'm just sayin'." Everyone laughed.

"We'll keep that in mind." Said Lola sarcastically. Destiny dressed fabulous like always, came over sitting beside her. She hugged her as she caressed her stomach.

"So if you don't mind, we'd like to take you and Dion out to lunch. In preparation for the big day."

"Okay. Sure."

"Well, I'm ready said Dion hurriedly placing on a pair of Jordan sneakers. David laughed at his son. "That's my boy." Dion helped Lola out of the chair and they headed out the door. Halfway through the meal, Julia decided to hit Lola with a questionnaire.

"So, Lauren my son has told us a lot about you. From what he has told us, he has grown very fond of you, and is in love with you. Dion smiled. Lola kissed his cheek. I would like to know what your plans are for the future. Being this will be our first grandchild, we'd love to be a part of their life and share those first memories."

"Well, I understand how close your family is and I would love to have you guys close to where we are. But, that's up to Dion and where his career goes. I love Dion and he is the best man I've ever known. You have raised a beautiful man, and I am honored to be a part of your family."

"We are happy our son has found someone to love. Who will be true and allow us to be a part of their lives we are a tight knit family, and we welcome you in with open arms." Said David. Lola smiled.

"Thank you. I have never had a family structure like this, and I would love to have this passed on to our baby."

After lunch, his parents went back to their suite and Dion and Lola were going back to their suite to get ready for the big night. Vita messaged stating she would meet up with them afterwards for cocktails, and apple cider for Lola.

The big night had arrived. Dion was dressed in a black Dolce & Gabbana suit which was accentuated with blue. He put on his watch and placed his necklace on his neck with Jesus pendant. Lola came out in a Dior dress that was strapless and flowing dress which room for her to move around in. She had her hair braided to the side which flowed into loose curls. She had on light makeup but accentuated it with red lipstick which made her lips pop, a look that Dion loved on her. She walked over to him. "You look amazing honey." Said Lola as she adjusted his shirt.

"Thank you. You look beautiful. He smiled looking into her eyes. I love you Lauren, and I'm happy to share this moment with you."

"I love you too baby."

"No, I *love* you Lauren. When I first met you, I knew you were different. You've become my best friend, you make me happy, you keep me grounded, you're beautiful, my prayer partner here and there, we can work on that you always have my back and I can't see my life without you."

Dion began to kneel down before her.

"What are you doing? D! Oh my God! Are you serious?" Lola began to cry, blushing as she turned her face away from his gaze. Dion smiled taking her hand.

"I want to spend my life with you. I want to make us one, because I can't imagine a day on this earth without you. Will you be my bae, sexy love, Monday and Friday, first lady, and better half... my wife. Lola began to smile at his ghetto impressions. He pulled out a black box opening it revealing a two carat solitaire ring in platinum setting. It was beautiful. Lauren Rose will you marry me? Lola began to cry. "Yes! Of course I will marry you Dion." He slid the ring on her finger, before standing to embrace her. Lola placed her arms around his neck kissing his lips. Her mascara had run all over her face. She begin to wipe her eyes, she saw the black on her fingers.

"Oh, I look like a big raccoon don't I?"

"No you're beautiful." He took his finger wiping away her mascara from her cheeks as he kissed her again.

The best moment of her life.

Once they arrived at Radio City Music hall. Lola sat beside his family. Julia smiled at Lola. "Welcome to our family, Lauren."

"How did you know?"

"Dion told us weeks ago, girl. Said Destiny. But, I definitely didn't think he was gonna pick this fly ass ring."

"Destiny!" said Julia. "Sorry, ma." Destiny admired the ring as the event started.

"The first draft pick for the San Diego Tigers…is Dion Girgis!" His family jumped up as he emerged on the stage. He put on his hat and raised his jersey in the air. The cameras panned over to Lola's wet face as she blew kisses to Dion. He smiled looking directly at her. Julia and David were in tears. David tried to hold back and be strong for family but he was ecstatic, his little boy had made it.

Afterwards Dion was emerged in so much press. He began to talk about how God made everything possible and he was grateful for his family. Lola finally had a moment to see him. He walked over kissing her.

"We're going to Cali, baby!"

"Congrats, Dion you did it! I'm so happy for you!" She kissed him again, as he hugged her tightly. That night everyone went out for drinks. When they arrived to the suite they made love and the next day they were on a flight to California.

Happy Wife/ Happy Life

Once in California, Lola was to find a place for her and Dion while he went to training. She had found a nice place in Pasadena. Three bedrooms, big backyard and pool, two car garage it was perfect. She decided she would put the money up for the house. With all of the loot she took from Uno she had well over enough to front the eight hundred thousand dollar plush Spanish villa. She was excited to tell Dion the news. She sent him a text message.

"I can't wait for you to see the new place, babe! It's freaking amazing!"

"Oh yeah, can't wait to see it. Love you beautiful." She left to purchase furniture and things for the house. Tonight they would stay at a suite and in the morning head to the house before he headed to training. Dion arrived home around eight that night, exhausted. Lola had prepared dinner Jerk chicken and rice. He walked inside kissed her lips and headed straight for the shower. After dinner they were sitting watching television. Lola began to tell him about the house.

"Baby it's gorgeous. I took pictures of it in my phone you have to see it."

"Oh yea, I trust your judgment."

She pulled out her phone to show him the pictures. "Yo, shit nice! You did good!"

"Thank you. I can't wait until I can decorate the baby room."

"I know we gotta do it right for our King."

"I know right. Me as a mommy… is a crazy thought you know. I've been reading every parenting book."

He smiled, wrapping his arm around her pulling her into him. He kissed her ear. "You will be an amazing mom Lauren. Me and You taking on the world!" She turned her face to his kissing his lips softly as he held her in his arms. Shortly drifting off to sleep, Lola snuggled in his arms his hands placed on her belly.

Several weeks later, they moved into their house. Today, was the big game and Dion was to start tonight. Vita had missed her flight out so, Lola was going to be cheering her baby on alone. She wore a jersey that she had custom made with Dion's number 4 on back and said *"the wifey"* paired with a pair of H&M tights and Jordan sneakers.

Dion came out in the third and led the team to a twenty point lead. Lola had nearly lost her voice from screaming so hard. They won the game and reporters swarmed Dion. He handled them all, before heading towards the showers. Once done he put on a black tee and sweats heading to meet Lo for dinner. He was summoned over for more press.

Lola held her belly waiting on Dion inside the backseat of the car. Her phone began to rang, she answered the phone knowing it was Dion. "Hi baby." She replied happily. The phone hung up. She looked at the phone and realized it was an unknown number. A text message came thru from Dion stating he would meet her at home, and he would call her once he was finished. Her driver looked back at Lola in the rear view mirror. "Shake Shack?"

She smiled. "You know it!" He smiled proceeding out of the parking lot. Once they arrived to Shake Shack and ordered Lola sat in backseat looking at her phone, knowing that Dion would be calling soon. Her phone began to ring loudly Displaying Hubby Facetime, she quickly put down her cup running her fingers thru her tresses. Before accepting. "Hey baby! You did amazing today?"

"Thank You Baby. Where are you?"

"You already know. She placed her cup in front of the screen. Dion shook his head placing the phone in cradle on his phone mount on the dashboard. I am so proud of you! I feel we should celebrate. You want to go out or I cook something?"

"You feel like making me some Jerk chicken and rice."

"Of course. I got you when we get home. How was your interviews?"

"It was alright you know they hit you with same questions over and over." He glanced in his rear view mirror, glancing out his driver window. Lola quickly noticed the concern on his face.

"Babe, what's up?"

"I'm good. Car, behind me. I think they been following me." He looked back in the rear view mirror, then back to the phone screen, a smile on this face. "I love you. How's my King?" Gun shots began to spray into the vehicle. The driver window shattered, glass flew all over Dion. Lola looked at the screen in horror. "BABY!! WHAT IS HAPPENING?" Bullets continue to spray the car as Dion slumped over in the seat. "OH

MY GOD! DION! DION?" Tires screeched as Lola stared at a blank screen.

*   *   *

Beauty for Ashes

The organist began to play, his eye is on the sparrow, and the room rang out in cries. It looked as if everyone in Pittsburgh had come out. Lola sat on the front row staring at the love of her life in the casket. He was dressed in all white, his hands at his side. He looked at peace. All she could hear was his voice ringing out over and over in her head.

"I love you. How's my King?"

She had cried so much she felt she ran out of tears. The team and coaches filled the room. His college friends and family all sat beside her. She had no words for anyone. She thought back to the concerned look on his face. It seemed so unreal. Who would do this to him? Was the question on everyone's mind. He was the fan favorite, clean cut, All-American guy. Why?

The more she thought about it the rage inside of her boiled over. She stood up from the pew and walked over to the casket. She looked at his face, as her tears finally emerged and fell unto his face.

"I love you baby. I love you Dion. She began to plead. She put her arms around him and kissed his face repeatedly. His mother began to sob louder, as everyone looked at Lauren. Wake up baby. Please, we want to see you." She pleaded as she hung unto the casket with her face on his chest. She began to sob loudly. The church clergy came to assist her back to her seat. Lola shrugged her off as she continued to rest her head back on his chest. Lola then felt two warm small hands on her back.

"Come on honey." She looked up seeing Vita. She was wearing a blonde wig and dark black shades, in a white Chanel suit. Lola hugged her tightly.

"I love him. Who would do this to him? Our baby… what are we going to do?!" Vita hugged her tightly as she walked her back to her seat. Lola cried in her arms as they proceeded to close the casket. Lola screamed out.

"NOO!!"

Vita tried to hold her back, as tears soon fell from behind her shades. After the funeral, Julia and family members asked Lauren if she wanted to stay in Pennsylvania, until the baby arrived. But, she obliged. She wanted space away from everyone. She had been questioned by police, and she had no idea or a clue of who would do this. She only wanted to lie in their house and look at pictures and video of her baby. The past weeks had been unbearable. She hadn't eaten a full meal, and everyone was worried for the safety of her and the baby. Vita came over and took her for a ride. She was in a black Mercedes, and had changed out of her suit to jeans and blazer. Lola sat in the car, distraught. "Vi, he's gone. My baby is gone!"

"I know you're hurt right now, Lo. But, you gotta get it together. You are carrying a baby, his baby. What would he think to see you acting like this? Have you fuckin' eaten anything?"

"I'm not hungry."

"You need to eat and man up bitch! We both know who did this!"

Lola looked confused. "What?"

"Lola, smell the roses get out of the fantasy. Uno did all this. You fucked him over, and he fucked you. You know he loved you, and he probably caught you and D on television, and set up the hit."

"You really think he did this?" said Lola.

"You *really* think he didn't? Why wouldn't he?"

"No. we've been over months ago."

"Lo, wake the fuck up! All I can say, they've been hitting my phone up leaving little messages." Lola began to ponder what Vita was saying. Uno did have the connections to arrange a hit like this. Did her actions actually lead to his death? She felt sick.

"So, we are about to head back out to Cali. You work on getting yourself back to health. Have this baby and were going to war. You down?"

"Hell yea." said Lola.

On September third, at six am, King Dion Girgis was born, weighing six lbs and eight inches long. He had chocolate brown hair and grey eyes. His eyes so piercing like his grandmother's, yet slanted like Lola's. He was the most beautiful baby she had ever seen. He laid in her arms looking into her eyes. She began to cry. She knew Dion would have been so happy, to meet his baby boy. She kissed his forehead. There was knocks at the door, she replied to enter. It was Vita followed by Dion's family. Julia's face lit up with a smile.

"Oh look at him. He's adorable." Destiny brought balloons and roses over to Lola's bedside. She hugged Lola and kissed her cheek. David smiled.

"He looks just like Dion did when he was born. Full of hair. Long arms." Lola smiled.

"What's his name?" said Julia as she rocked him in her arms.

"King Dion Girgis." Julia held back her tears.

"Our little king, he is."

Vita came over sitting on her bed. "How are you feeling?"

"I'm okay. Did you get everything set up for me at the house?" said Lola. "Yep. Baby room is set and everything."

"Good."

"So, how are you doing Lauren? Do you need help with King?"

"I think I'm okay. Just going to take it easy until me and King get a schedule going." David brought King over to Lola. He saw the picture of Dion beside the bed. He was sitting on the bed, candid shot, with a smile on his face. He truly missed his son. He looked at King's face he saw his son, and tears began to form in his eyes. The family stayed for two hours before heading to their hotel. Vita came over sitting beside the bed.

"So, you ready to go to Atlanta, and get at his ass."

"Vi, I can't leave King. Besides, I can't put him at risk like that."

"So, you're going to let this shit slide? He killed your man!" Screamed Vita.

"Vi, I'm a mother now and King has to be my number one priority right now. I need to establish a safe environment for him."

"What are you going to do for money? I know they have King a trust fund and SSI, but you can't maintain that house without something to fall on."

"Vi, I will figure it out. I am just in no condition to do that shit right now, ya know? Besides, why are you so anxious to peel this motherfucker?"

"I haven't talked to Mill in months now. None of his family knows where he is or anything. I think Uno has something to do with that. Besides, they popped Dion! Lola, you owe it to him."

"I owe my son, a happy life, that's it. It's his first day on this earth I don't want him around such negativity and hatred. Now, one day I will address this and get closure. But, right now, my son is my priority."

"So that's how it is bitch? Fine. Take care of King. Congratulations." Vita stormed out of the hospital. Lola shook her head as she looked down at her precious baby boy. He smiled gazing into her eyes. She kissed his lips.

"Just me and you lovie."

A Hustler's Ambition

Months later, Vita's prediction proved to be right. Between paying the expensive bills at her dream home, food, and maintaining she was getting low on cash. The money King received from Dion's estate did help, but she only used that money on him. She never spent any for her up keep, only on bills. She hadn't gotten her hair done in months. Today King had woke up at seven, which was early for Lola, being that she had been up the night before making plans for Christmas.

She placed a bottle in the bottle warmer as she rocked King in her arms. He was a peaceful baby. He loved to smile and he was a mixture of his parent's features. She made sure she kept as less drama around him as possible. She read him books, took him to museums and spent almost every minute with him. Lola always showed him pictures of Dion. His room was adorned with football theme and the number four. She turned on the television as she fed him. A commercial came on about Vegas showgirls. Her eyes glanced over the mountain of bills which sat on the table, she looked down at King her mind racing with thoughts. Maybe she should check it out. She decided to drive to Vegas tonight. She hadn't heard from Vita in a while, she wondered what she was up to. She called her cell, it rang four times before she answered.

"Hello."

"Hello stranger. Are you still mad at me?"

"Nope. I'm good. How are you?"

"I'm okay. Maintaining." Said Lola as she began to burp King.

"How's my god baby?"

"Oh, he's just fine, getting bigger every day, looking like Dion's twin. Lola chuckled. So where are you living now? You ever find Mill?"

"Well, I'm living in Detroit. But, I'm in Vegas with my new friend. Yea, I found Mill, he's living in Philly with his woman."

"WHAT?"

"Yea, when I was looking around worried about him, he had moved on to some bitch."

"Oh, my god! How do you feel about that? I mean, y'all were together awhile."

"Yea, but fuck him. I heard Uno may be moving into his house on west coast."

"Oh yeah. Well it doesn't matter because I'm going to have to leave here anyway. My bills are piling up. You were right, so I have to figure out something else for us."

"So what are you about to do?"

"Well, I was thinking of driving out to Vegas and maybe see about dancing?"

"Are you serious?" said Vita her voice rising.

"It's good money and besides I can't see myself getting a new nigga right now. It's still too early and this way I can support my son myself."

"Well, if that's what you want to do, no judgment. But, who is going to watch King at night?"

"I'll figure it out. Maybe, I can get a good nanny?"

"Look come here today and I'll stay a few days to help you out while you get things together."

"You would do that?"

"You're my sister." Said Vita affectionately. Lola smiled that almost brought her to tears. She just knew that Vita would hate her for turning her back on her when she needed help finding Mill. Here she was lonely in Cali thinking she had no support system and Vita still had her back.

"Okay. I'm coming tonight now let me pack up King's things and I'll be there."

"You don't need to pack anything but his bottles. I got you guys when you get here, okay."

"You don't have to do that Vi." said Lola sympathetically.

"Just let me help you girl. You know me, shit, I wanna spoil my god baby."

Lola laughed. She told her she would pack up the BMW and would be on her way. She put King on a blue Ralph Lauren Polo onesie and matching khaki shorts and tan Ralph Lauren loafers. She brushed his curly locks and placed a newsboy hat to match. He smiled looking at Lola in his carrier as she pulled out a Dior dress. She hadn't been dressed up in a while and she had lost a lot of weight. She was smaller now than before King. She threw out her suitcase and threw a few things inside and in an hour they were on the road. In over four and a half hours they arrived in Vegas. She pulled over to change King again and feed him.

"Hey were here."

"Damn, that was quick. Well, I'm at the Four Seasons. I'll meet you in the lobby."

"Okay."

"Don't worry about room I already got that taken care of."

"What? Come on girl, you don't have to."

"Lo, just bring your ass. I got this." Lola laughed deciding to not argue with Vita. When she arrived valet parked the car and she carried King in his carrier. They gathered her bags as she walked into the hotel. She tried to pull her hair back out of her face. She had pulled it back into a neat tight ponytail. Her makeup was light, but she had on red lipstick. As she walked towards the seats, she looked ahead seeing a slender woman walking her way with long black hair. She looked flawless, expensive shades and long Versace sheer dress that flowed behind her as she walked in her direction. She realized as she got closer it was Vita. She had lost a lot of weight. Her once round face was now sunken in, her curves still there , but it wasn't the Vita Lola knew. Her breast which were once a DD, were a C and her arms were thin. She removed her shades as she approached Lola. "Well, hello Bitch."

"Hey! Look at you!" said Lola happily.

"Yea, I know I've lost some weight since you last saw me. But, look at you, Bitch, you look fabulous. Like, you never had a baby."

"Well, thanks. But, between the stress of Dion and post-partum, I've been a fucking mess."

"Well, girl you look great. Need a little Vita touch to this hair, but you're good baby girl."

Lola laughed as King began to squirm in his carrier. Lola bent down to pick him up. "Oh, my God! He is so fucking adorable Lo. He looks just like you and Dion."

"Thank you. You want to hold him?"

"Um, yea. give me my god baby." Vita laughed picking up King. He looked into her eyes and smiled. "Ooh, look at his eyes. He is going to be a heartbreaker, Lo. What have you been feeding this boy?"

Lola laughed. "He may be a future pro baller like his father." Lola looked into his face and thought about Dion. It always sent a feeling inside, that made her feel awkward. "Let's, get you guys up to your room."

Lola followed Vita up to the suite. The room was gorgeous. Plush furniture, crib, and stocked with brand new baby supplies. Lola was overwhelmed. "Thank you so much Vi. I appreciate this so much." "No problem. So it is paid up for the next two months, until you get things situated. Do you have a plan of which place you trying to work at?"

"Um, no. I don't even think I have what it takes."

"Well, you shouldn't do either one of those petty ass jobs. You're too fly for that. Now, my friend's right hand man is looking for a friend, and I told him about you."

"Vita, I told you I'm not ready to date. Besides I don't want just anybody around King. No offense. But I can't have another Uno. Beating my ass and raping me and shit. I'll kill a nigga that fucks with my child."

"Well, if this is what you want to do. I got your back. But, I was thinking something better. How about we go into business together."

"What kind of business, Vi?"

"The game. I mean why not? We smarter than these dumb niggas." Vita placed her hands on her hips.

"Too risky. I have things to lose now. I don't want to sound like an ungrateful bitch. But, I was adopted Vita. I was left on steps in a basket, I don't want my son to end up like that. I want to try this the legal way, have as much of a normal life that I can give him. Then, if this doesn't work, I do other things. But, I at lease want to try."

"Alright. I feel you. But, don't get caught up in this Vegas lifestyle. Because it's easy for a bitch to start turning tricks and getting fucked up out here."

"I'm only in it for the money. I know with this I can be guaranteed money that will help me and my baby live comfortably until the next step. Then I can open my own business or something."

"Nothing wrong with dreaming. But, I'm living for today." Vita pulled out her handy mint box. She poured a handful and swallowed hard. Lola was definitely going to have to look into a nanny.

That day Lola went to several different clubs. Half the owners were pervs, they wanted to sample her goodies and continued to ask her what drug was she on. She became defeated. She couldn't see herself letting these men touch her for a job. As she decided to head back to the room she saw a club, the Doll House. It had a pink sign in bright lights, the club looked like a casino from the outside. It looked classy and upscale. She decided to go inside. She sprayed on Dolce & Gabbana perfume. Lola glanced down at her watch, six pm, she walked up to security. They looked her up and down as she twirled her hair on her finger. "I need to see a manager or owner." "Okay. Gonna need to check you sexy." She placed her hands up as the guard ran the metal detector across her body as he ran it across her back, it felt as if he moved slower. Lola bit her lip. He stopped and faced her again. Go inside and speak to Kori at the entrance and she'll put you back to Gary. She smiled walking into the club. When she walked to the desk, she saw a beautiful blonde woman wearing a suit sitting behind the register. The register was surrounded by fish tanks and pink lights. Lola looked around in awe. "How you doing honey? She said, you needed to see Gary?"

"Yes. I guess. I'm looking for a job."

She stood up and looked Lola over. "Can you turn around sweetie?" Lola turned around slowly, the woman smiled. "I think you definitely have the look that were about at the doll house. You're exotic, smoking body and clean. You definitely have the job."

"What? Who are you? I thought I needed to see Gary?"

"Not really. Gary is my husband and I know what he likes. I tend to hire most of the ladies here. You will give him a heart attack." The woman laughed. Lola couldn't help but laugh with her. "My name is Kori Stephens. Yours?"

"Lola Dion."

"Okay, let me show you around." said Kori. Kori showed her around the club. It was immaculate and clean. Beautiful separate rooms for private dances, pink and black decor. A few girls were coming to the stage: Jazz and Kitty. They were two black girls who were young and beautiful. "Kitty is one of our trainers. She does a few nights a week at the peep show. You need some training definitely check out her training class." Kitty had a long blonde wig and a thong which was pink and lace. Thigh high boots and fishnets, she climbed her way to the top of the pole and began to glide down with ease. As if it didn't bother her at all, she twirled herself upside down while fanning her legs open. The music changed to Jay-Z, Lola was in awe. No way she could do all of that. Kori took her backstage to show her the dressing rooms. Kori then led her to her office. "Well, normally we would have you perform for us. But, I like what I see and I'm pretty sure you really need the work. So, whatever needs help, we will work on it. You're gorgeous and you will be a great asset here. So, how about you start tomorrow night, we'll put you on stage with another girl and then that will let us know where we can blend you in."

"Umm, okay."

"Think about your gimmick and costume. Wax, and I'll see you at six tomorrow."

"Okay."

They shook hands before Lola headed towards the door. She didn't know it would be this easy. She headed towards the parking lot. She had her first job.

Lola was ecstatic about the job yet nervous. This was going to be her new meal ticket. What if she was garbage? She didn't know the first thing about dancing. Her nerves began to run wild she decided to call Vita and they needed to hit the mall immediately to find the perfect costume. Lola went upstairs to pack up King and they were headed to the mall. Vita told her she didn't have any doubts about Lola finding a job, she knew she would get one. Vita began to rant about Lola's costume should be something sexy, yet a good gimmick. She began to spit out costumes as a cheerleader, football player. Lola's mind began to drift away in a daydream, thinking of a perfect costume. She decided on wearing leather, toting a prop gun and being a natural bad ass. It would be something she could portray fairly easily and she had endless prop ideas to choose from. At the end of the day she had purchased a fedora, gun holster, thong and net tank top.

The next morning Lola went to the gym with King in his carrier. As she was walking back towards the car she spotted Kitty across the parking lot walking over to a Range Rover. She was wearing a pink sports bra and matching tights. Her hair was honey blond and cut in a cute pink pixie cut. Lola yelled out to her. "Kitty!" She signaled for her to come over to her. She saw Kitty's resistance at first, but when she saw the carrier her fear subsided. Kitty walked towards her. Lola could see her coke bottle figure sway in the wind. She was sexy. Lola fixed her wife beater and pulled down her Nike shorts over her butt. Kitty walked over her phone dangling in her hand. "May I help you?" said Kitty her voice polite yet hood. "Yea. I'm Lola, I will start at the Doll House tonight and Kori told me to get with you about getting a routine?"

"You're gonna be working at Doll House? You're pretty." "Thank you." Kitty looked into the carrier at King who was looking back into her eyes.

"He's so cute. But, if you have some time now we can step in the studio and I can show you a little something."

"Oh okay. That's fine." Kitty showed her into the dance studio which sat beside the gym. There was two poles in the middle of the floor and mirrors everywhere. Kitty walked over to the sound system, she turned on an instrumental dance mix. "So, show me what you got, mama?"

Lola suddenly felt nervous. She had never put on a show for a female. Well, for Vita last night, but Kitty intimidated her this was her career. Lola handed King his pacifier as she headed for the pole. She began to rock her hips slowly to the song, she placed her fingers through her hair and shook her hair out freely as she touched her toes and began to make her ass bounce. She twirled around on the pole, while walking on her tiptoes sexily. Kitty smiled. She stopped the music. "You're naturally sexy so you need to use your eyes and hands more. Guys, like exotic bitches. You're all of that." Kitty began to bat her eyes while touching her own body sensually. Lola followed her lead and began to mimic. Kitty went towards the pole and began to show her a routine. Two hours later, Lola was in the hotel room, exhausted. Around four, she packed her outfit for tonight. There was two knocks at the door, it was nanny Vita. She brought a bottle of Moet. They popped it open to take the edge off of tonight. Vita pulled out her pill box and asked Lola if she wanted any. She said no. After three drinks she headed for the club.

The Fast Life

Once at the club Lola was escorted back to the dressing rooms. Breasts and asses everywhere, different nationalities all beautiful. Lola went to sit at the first open mirror. She placed her duffel bag on the floor and looked at her reflection in the mirror. Although she was buzzed, her nerves began to get the best of her. Would she really go through with this? Just as her thoughts began to get the best of her, a woman appeared beside her. She looked her body up and down. Bronzed honey skin, round face, brown bright eyes and pink pouty lips. She looked possibly Bajan. Lola's eyes soon went down to her D breast which sat perky with a jeweled tassel hanging from them, and a black g-string, leather stiletto boots. She shifted her weight unto her right arm as she leaned on the counter. "So, you're the new girl huh? She asked half sarcastically. My name is Poison. You're going to be on stage with me tonight. What's your name?" "Lola."

"Maybe you should go by Lolita, that's a better name then using your real name."

"Well, Lola is not my real name and it is the name that I'm going to use." Poison rolled her eyes.

"Got a little mouth on you huh? Good. Maybe it will be good for something, we go on in fifteen." Poison stormed away. Lola watched her walk away, two more women came over to her.

"You told that bitch! I'm MaiTai and this is Butterscotch." MaiTai was Hawaiian, Long full black hair and she was wearing a cheerleading skirt that revealed her ass. Butterscotch was mixed, possibly Puerto Rican, about

5"7", DD breast and round ass. She was wearing a netted catsuit, revealing everything. "Hi, I'm Lola." "You better get ready girl. You're up after us." Said Butterscotch with a strong Spanish accent. "Oh, okay. Thanks." Lola stood up taking off her joggers. Butterscotch looked at Lola, she was wearing a lace body suit, revealing everything. She sat down applying gloss to her lips. Butterscotch came over with a black wig with Chinese bang. "Put this on."

"Why?"

"Because, you don't want these niggas knowing what you look like. You're gonna be a fucking star." Butterscotch smiled. Something in her smile seemed genuine and Lola decided to trust her she put on the wig.

"I have the perfect lip kit for you." Said MaiTai. MaiTai proceeded to help do her make up. After five minutes, Lola glanced at her reflection stunned by the quick transformation. Butterscotch and MaiTai headed towards the stage. Lola clutched her fingers around a bottle of Grey Goose pursing it to her lips.

She could hear the crowd applauding as they called out their names. Poison stepped in front of her sashaying her body to the hip hop mix. Lola walked out calmly her hand on her hip. She began to think about little King waiting for her at home, she looked out at the crowd and the men were lined around the stage. Staring at her body like hungry wolves, she thought about Dion. Fuck it. She needed this money. She glided down to the end of the stage falling to her knees. There was a mid-forties business executive, drooling over her as he poured his bottle of champagne. Lola picked up the bottle put it up to her lips slowly, letting her tongue play with the tip. She then shook up the bottle as she moved her body up and down on her knees pouring champagne all over herself. The guys began to shout as her perky nipples began to peer through her lace. They began throwing money all over her. She squatted down as she popped her ass to the music. Caressing all over her body, she sat the bottle in between her legs as if she was gonna ride it. She now had them foaming at her feet. Poison was on the back pole shaking her ass to a few onlookers, but Lola had everyone's full attention. She handed the bottle back to the man. She quickly bent completely over, making her ass clap as Kitty had taught her. Men placed money in her boots. She walked slowly over to the pole, making sure her eyes said everything. She wrapped one of her legs around the pole and let her body dangle as she fingered her mouth. Poison looked over at Lola's spectacle. She climbed off the pole, taking off her thong. She crawled towards the end of the stage and began to spread her legs open while shaking her ass in the air. Lola continued on the pole and in seconds, her lace camisole was on the floor. She let her body slide slowly down the pole, the guys cheered and shouted their eyes glued to her body. She began to make her ass clap again as eyes shifted towards her. The song was over and Lola realized her finale could make or break her. Poison looked over at her as she smiled knowing she had this show in the bag.

Lola strutted over to Poison as she sat on her knees. She laid Poison down as she caressed her body she guided her hands softly over her. Poison smiled feeling Lola's energy, she became turned on. Poison began to massage Lola's ass, as she crawled up to Poison's lips. Poison kissed Lola's breast, as she gyrated as if she was riding a man. Lola then squatted over her face. Poison was wrapped in the moment, began to kiss Lola's vagina. The guys went crazy throwing more stacks unto the stage. Lola looked back at them with a seductive smirk, she then slapped Poison in the face and collected her money as she walked off the stage. The crowd went crazy. MaiTai and Butterscotch were waiting by the stage. "You are gonna have your own segment, bitch. You killed that shit!" Butterscotch put her hand out for a hi-five. Lola smiled returning the favor and taking off the wig. She was exhausted. She threw on her sweats and top. MaiTai walked over. "We normally go to Nino's to eat breakfast, you should come?" "I have to get home to my baby." "Oh, ok. We all understand. We have kids too. Maybe tomorrow, you can hang." "Maybe." Lola stuffed the money in her bag as it fell onto the floor. Moments later, Poison emerged from the stage. Too embarrassed to make eye contact with Lola, she ran her fingers thru her hair to hide her face. "I guess your mouth is good for something too." Poison didn't say a word as she walked back to her mirror. Everyone laughed. Kori soon appeared and everyone became quiet. "Lola that was quite a performance." "Thank you." She said nervously.

"The crowd loved you. You're edgy, sexy and daring. We're going to give you your own segment. Meet up with Kitty tomorrow to work on a routine."

"Oh, wow. Thanks!"

"We are going to have a party for Gary this weekend everyone is invited. Here's your check and you start tomorrow night solo." "Thank you so much!" Kori hugged her and then walked away. Lola looked down at the check. Three thousand dollars.

"So, we'll definitely see you for breakfast tomorrow." Said MaiTai. "Okay." "Congrats!" Lola took her bag and headed out the door. Security walked her over to her car as she placed her bag in the trunk. The security smiled,

"You one fine ass woman, Lola. Damn, I'd love to see you outside of club."

"Sorry, boo. Not happening." She replied as she slid behind the driver seat. When she arrived to her suite, Vita was passed out on her King sized bed. King lay beside her swaddled in his blanket. Lola took a shower and came to bed. She looked over at her lovie, kissing his cheek. She poured the money unto the bed and began to count. Six thousand dollars. Not bad. Nine thousand in one night, things weren't going to be bad at all.

Several months later, Lola was a regular at the club. She had two sets a night and was bringing home thousands of dollars a night. Lola changed her shift to only three nights a week, Thursday Friday and Saturday. Butterscotch and Maitai, better known as Selena and Ana, had become her good friends. Lola had moved out of the hotel into a cute townhouse, with garage and middle class neighborhood. She had met a new guy Vincent bka Vin while at a celebrity party at Palms hotel. He was Italian, six feet tall, black hair, cocky from California. What attracted Lola to him was the fact that he dressed in fly tailored suits. Vin owned a promotion business and always showered Lola and King with the best. Lola was firm and cautious in not having King around Vin their relationship was new and she didn't want King around anyone. King's first birthday was coming up, Lola decided she wanted to take him to Pennsylvania to see his family. King was crawling across the floor as Lola changed into a strapless dress. She smiled seeing how big her little King had become. Her phone beeped with numerous messages.

"Lola we can't wait to see Little King from his pictures he is getting so big! Call us soon as possible." Said his grandmother.

Lola smiled at King throwing him in the air he smiled brightly, showing his gums. "You want to see your Nana? Huh? You want to go to Pennsylvania baby?" He laughed loudly as she made raspberry noises on his stomach. He grabbed her hair. She sat him on her lap and responded to all of her messages. The last message was from Vita. It simply stated "Come out to Jersey."

She responded "You know I can't come to Jersey right now. But maybe once I come to get King from Pennsylvania; I'll stop thru."

"Sure, bitch. I haven't seen you in forever." She responded snappily.

Lola laughed out loud and decided then that she would go see her friend. She missed her. She heard keys jingle at the door, it was King's nanny, Janice, who was highly recommended from a child care agency, that all of the girls at the club used. Janice was a sweetheart. She was Cuban late fifties and adored King.

"Good morning darling!" she shouted as she hung her jacket in the closet. King perked up seeing her walking in his direction. He reached his arms out to her.

"Good morning Janice. I have a few errands to run and a date today. So, I would need you to stay over tonight."

"No problem, Miss Lola."

"Thank you." She handed King over to Janice. She began to speak to him in Spanish. He laughed. Lola kissed him before she hurried upstairs. She called Vin to see if their lunch plans were still on. He said yes and that he couldn't wait to see her. She went in the bathroom changing again into a Versace inspired dress with gold chains and a lion's head print all over. It hugged her every curve and stopped right below her ass. She put a bikini in her overnight bag and outfit. Minutes later she was heading towards Café Chateau a trendy restaurant south of the strip. Once there valet parked the car and she headed inside. The server took her to the table where Vin was seated wearing an Armani Suit, he smiled bright which made her smile. He stood up to hug her. His six foot, two hundred and ten pound body enveloped her frame. He smelled good like always and his expensive Cartier watch glistened on his wrist. "Hello Baby. How are you?" He said as he looked into her eyes.

"I'm good. How did the promotion deal go?"

"Good. Made a good endorsement deal and we are having Sasha Money at party tonight."

"Sasha Money! She's huge. That's amazing."

Sasha Money was a triple threat. Pop star, rapper turned actress. She was on every magazine cover as the body to have, face of the year, and hottest recording artist. Lola was star struck and she hadn't met her yet.

"Party is in LA. So, I was thinking we take a flight over there and stay for a few days."

"Babe… I can't stay a few days. I have to have King situated." Said Lola affectionately. He smiled.

He placed a stack of money on the table. "Give that to the Nanny. I need you in L.A. with me. He reached across the table and kissed her face. How could she refuse? She looked at the stack of cash it had to be about eight thousand dollars. That would be way over enough to keep Janice for a few days with King. It had been the longest she would be away from King and in her care alone. But she trusted Janice. Vin smiled at her.

"So, we'll leave in maybe two hours? Will that be enough time to have King situated?"

"Um… I guess." She said half seriously. "How much should I pack?"

"Nothing, just bring you. I have everything else covered for you." He said with a smile.

From the inside looking in; it would seem like dejavu, jet setting lifestyle that Uno had once shown her. But, Lola had somehow buried the scars Uno has once left on her. Vin had never lifted a finger to her let alone raise his voice. She felt he was genuine. She was happy to be going to Los Angeles, for she loved the parties and shopping. But it felt a bit awkward to return without her ace Vita. She began to wonder if she was available to go.

After a four course meal, and a stuffed stomach. She hurried home. Janice was in the living room folding King's laundry as she listened to her favorite Motown favorites. King began to jump up and down as Lola approached him. "Welcome Home miss Lola. Can I get you anything?"

"Oh no, Janice I'm fine. She replied as she picked King up out the playpen. She began to kiss his lips. His drool trickled down her lips. Lola saw Dion in his eyes. That warm smile and laugh that she had fell in love with in his father. She decided she couldn't leave him home with Janice for a few days.

"Janice, do you have any plans the next few days?"

"No, ma'am. Is there something I can do for you?"

"I am going to Los Angeles for a few days and would like you and King to come along with me?"

"Um... sure, Miss. When would you like to leave?"

"We're leaving in a couple of hours. I will get you a suite and you can watch King during day."

"Okay."

"Everything on me. Double pay. Is that okay?" said Lola.

"Yes. I will go get my things and be back here in an hour if that's okay?"

"Oh, thank you. That's fine."

"Okay."

Janice placed the clothes she was folding in King's basket. "I got it." Said Lola walking towards the basket. She put King back in the playpen and began packing his things for the trip. In her haste of packing she then thought about did she want King to meet Vin yet. He had been sweet, but King had not seen any man in his life something she prided herself on doing. She sat back on the ottoman that was in his walk in closet. Maybe he shouldn't go? Her mind began to race, she decided to call Vita. She would always have the perfect answer good or bad. It rang three times before she picked up.

"Oh, what the hell do I owe the honor of speaking to your ass twice in one day?"

Lola laughed out loud. "What's that supposed to mean?"

"Whatever bitch. You only call me when you got some crazy ass shit going down. Just threw me to the side like chopped fucking liver."

"Vi, don't even go there! You know you're my best fucking friend, you're beyond that my sister. Besides you don't speak to me much anyway either! Wassup with that?!"

"Girl, boo. I'm always checking in to see about my boo-thing King. Now, you on the other hand... not too much!" They both laughed.

"Well, anyway, my new guy I'm seeing wants to take me out to Los Angeles for a few days. I don't know about leaving King at home with Nanny. I mean for that many days, I have never left him alone. What should I do?"

"I mean is she good peoples? You did the background I'm assuming on this chick?"

"Hell yea! I just feel some sort of way leaving King in Vegas for a week without me. I mean sending him to Pittsburgh or having him with you, I know y'all won't let anything happen to my luvie. But, I'm a little nervous. So, I told the nanny I can bring her with us. Should I?"

"I think you should go. I haven't heard anything about Uno lately... But, you can feel this nanny out and see if in future you can leave him with her, for long periods of time. Leave him with her for like a whole day and see how you feel while there. What's going on in LA? Damn, I miss LA!"

"Sasha Money is there. He's in promotions, so he has a few deals going on."

"That sounds good. Is he treating you right?"

"Yea. This is totally different. No, Uno bullshit here."

"Okay, I'm happy for you. So, when you leaving for LA?"

"In a couple hours."

"Do you know where you're staying yet?"

"No, but I think he said something about The Ritz-Carlton. So, might be there."

"Alright. So take the baby with you and the nanny and call me once y'all get settled to let me know everything is ok."

"Okay."

"Talk to you later." They hung up and Lola continued to scurry around getting all of King's belongings. She put on a pair of ripped jeans over a Celiné Tank. Her hair pulled back in a ponytail. Christian Louboutin flats, in mommy mode. Minutes later Janice came back to the house with her suitcase in tow. Janice took King's Louis Vuitton Luggage along with his stroller. In fifteen minutes they were headed out the door. Lola's phone rang it was Vin.

"Hello love. Are you ready?"

"Yea, we're on our way to airport." Said Lola.

"We?"

"Yes. I'm bringing my baby and nanny. I decided I don't want to be too far away from them. I will get them a suite at wherever we are staying, is that okay?"

"Oh that's fine. I got a private plane so there is plenty of room and no need for you to pay for suite. I'll have it covered."

"No, I'll pay for it." Lola pleaded.

"Nonsense. I have it covered. I look forward to meeting little King."

"Well, we will be seeing you soon."

"Okay. Talk to you soon Bella." Lola smiled hanging up the phone. She wasn't going to let Vin pay for suite, but since he obliged she decided to let him handle it since he was persistent. Once they reached the airport. Lola saw Vin's Maserati parked up off the runway with his team. He was in a white linen shirt over dark denim jeans. She had never seen him dressed so relaxed. It was sexy and edgy to her. Janice went to get their luggage and bags out the car. Men came over taking the bags for her. Lola took King out of his seat. He was exhausted from the ride and she knew in moments he would be sleeping. Lola walked over to Vin. "Is this the little guy I've heard so much about?" He smiled as he touched King's fingers.

"King this is Vin, mommy's friend. Say hi." King placed his hand over his eyes and gave a halfhearted wave. Vin chuckled. "Someone's tired eh? He's handsome bella." Vin kissed her cheek. "Oh, Vin... this is Janice, his nanny."

"Pleasure to meet you. If you need anything while there let me know. I will be sure you get it. Don't ask Lola!" said Vin with a smile.

Janice laughed. "Certainly sir."

"Let us be on our way." He extended his arm for them all to board the plane.

An hour later they were heading in two Yukon's to the hotel. Lola and Vin in one and King and Janice in the other. Vin told Janice anywhere she wanted to go, that would be her driver. They were to stay at the Ritz-Carlton and he had got Janice a suite two rooms down from theirs. On the ride to the room he had been on call after call. He told Lola he would be busy for the next few hours handling business, but gave her a couple stacks of money to go shopping with the driver. She said of course. She went down to Janice & King's suite to get King settled in. Once he was relaxed with Janice she went to her suite, to change clothes. There was a loud knock at the door.

BOOM. BOOM. BOOM. She crept to the door, wondering who this could be. "Who is it?"

"Housekeeping!"

Lola didn't bother to look through peephole. She opened the door seeing Vita at the door. She was thin, her hair blonde and pulled to one side. Her breasts were spilling out of her orange long flowing dress. Her face piled with makeup, flawless nevertheless but different than the Vita she knew.

"Hola Bitch!"

"Vi, what the hell are you doing here?" She replied as she hugged her tightly.

"I was in LA. I was going to actually surprise you in Vegas before I head back to east coast. But, since you said you would be out here, I decided to check on you."

"Oh wow! I'm so happy to see you. Seems like I haven't seen you in forever!"

"I know. You making mad money in Vegas and you just said fuck Vi." Vita walked in and Lola closed the door behind her. Lola looked at Vita's round ass, it was still juicy like always. But her shoulders and arms were noticeably thin. "So, what's going on with you? Did you get new boobs?" said Lola.

"Yea bitch. I woke up one day and those motherfuckers were looking a hot ass mess. So, I told my nigga I'm too pretty for this shit. So meet my new ones!" Vita began to massage her breasts.

"They look really good though. Not fake or anything."

"Yea. As much as they cost they better look fucking flawless." They both laughed. Lola sat down on the couch. "So why were you in Los Angeles?" said Lola.

"Well, Rock has a meeting with his people and we were out here."

"Oh who's Rock? What business he in?"

"Rock, guy I've been fucking with. He's cool, mid-level nigga, into Coke and pills."

"Okay. Is he good to you?" said Lola.

"He's alright. He doesn't put his hands on me. But, we all have our fucking demons." Said Vita as she looked away.

"Well, you be safe, take care of yourself. Lola replied looking affectionately in Vita's eyes. It's good to see you."

"You too." Said Vita as she scratched her arm feverishly.

Lola looked at her confused. "You good?"

"Yea. I'm great! Couldn't be fucking better. So where's King?" said Vita standing up.

"He's asleep in their suite." Said Lola.

"Well do you want to go shopping? Let's get out of this fucking room!"

"Let me grab my purse." Lola stood up heading towards the bedroom. Vita began to fan herself. She went into her purse and began to search for a quick fix she pulled out a little vial she carried of a cocaine cocktail. It was low. She took two blows and wiped her nose. Lola came back out the room and Vita was laid back on the couch touching her breast.

"What are you doing?" said Lola playfully.

"Nothing. You ready? Do you have a driver? I have one if you don't. Let's go! I'm hungry are you?" said Vita energetically. She got up off the couch walking quickly to the door. Lola looked at her friend, something was definitely up with Vita. She just hoped it wasn't what she suspected.

*   *   *

Once back from a day of shopping Lola and Vita were in the car heading to grab a quick bite to bring home. Vita became very quiet she began looking frantically out the window and staring at Lola as if she didn't know who she was. "Vi, are you good?" said Lola.

"I'm good. Why you asking me that? You want to fuck me or something?" said Vita defensively.

"What? You look high as a fucking kite! Are you still popping pills?"

"No, I don't do that shit no more. I'm good. I'm just exhausted."

Lola had over ten bags, Vita had two. Normally when they shopped together they would share a fitting room. Today, Vita was distant. She tried on nothing and bought random items. A scarf and a pair of clearance rack Gucci heels that were green with hot orange buttons. Quite tacky and not at all Vita's taste. Lola looked over at her again. Lola looked at Vita's legs they were black and blue, her knees looked horrible. Her toe nail polish a dingy nude that it looked like she did herself. She felt sorry for her friend, she was definitely using. "Vi, I love you." Said Lola as she laid on her shoulder. Vita looked down at her. Her eyes glossy and looking at her up close, Lola could see the dark spots on her once full beautiful lips, were now cracked and dry. Vita put her hand on Lola's shoulder. "Bitch, you still not getting my cookies. But, I love you too." Once back at the room Lola and Vita went their separate ways and were to meet up the next day before Vita left town. Lola sat and thought about how today Vita was a complete different person than who she spoke on phone with earlier. She couldn't believe Vita had let herself go. She had to do something for her friend.

Hours later, Lola was dressed for the party. Vin came into the bathroom as Lola fixed her makeup with a bottle of Moet in his hand. He looked great in his Gucci suit, he had a cigar in his mouth and began to kiss on Lola's nude shoulders. She had bought a red strapless Herve dress that had her breasts spilling out. She looked gorgeous. Vin began to kiss her ear and neck. "You look stunning baby." He said looking at their reflection in the mirror.

"Thank you." Said Lola as she continued to fix her hair.

"I got something for you." He placed the bottle on the counter. He reached deep into his pocket. Lola smiled excited to see what the gift could be. He handed her the jewelry box. She ripped the top off revealing a diamond bracelet.

"It's beautiful! You didn't have to do this!" said Lola as she kissed his lips.

"Anything for my baby. Soon a diamond will sit on that finger." He pointed to her ring finger. She laughed. "Oh really."

He smiled kissing her lips. "Really. No more working at the fucking club you'll be my muse." He kissed her lips passionately, Lola could taste the Moet on his lips. It began to turn her on and from the bulge forming in his pants. So was he. Lola was curious. She sat on top of the counter bringing his body into hers. He grabbed her chin kissing her lips his other arm rested on the mirror as he moved down to her breasts. "Wait… Let me take this off." She said as she began to try to unhook the dress.

"Fuck it baby. I'll buy you another one!" She began to unbutton his pants as he threw off his jacket. He placed his fingers up her dress as she unbuttoned his shirt. Lola moaned as he began to his fingers played in between her thighs. Lola kissed his chest and stomach as she inched her hands down inside his boxers. She smiled sweetly as she looked over his seven and half inches. He smiled picking her up taking her over to the bed. She hadn't been with anyone since Dion. Vin put a condom on before sliding in. She let out a loud moan as he grinded slowly on top of her, his arms bulging over her shoulders. She looked into his eyes and she thought about Dion. She tried to shake the visual of Dion out of her mind. "I'm sorry babe." She shouted out loud. Vin was a beast, he stretched one of her legs over his shoulder as he inched deeper. She then pinned Vin down and began to ride him backwards cowgirl as she continue to see Dion in her mind. She fought back the tears as she continued to ride him and he grabbed her waist. "Shit! Pussy good. Fuck!" He then threw Lola on her stomach thrusting his dick in her pussy from the back. She screamed out as he slapped her ass. He began to pull her hair and grab her neck from behind. He moaned as he took his dick out and began to perform fellatio on her. Lola clawed the sheets. Twenty minutes later. She lay beside Vin. Both covered in sweat. He kissed her breasts. Before getting out the bed. "You're a wild girl." He said with a mischievous grin. He went into the bathroom. Lola got up to take a shower. "Are we still going to party?" said Lola jokingly.

"Yea... said Vin from behind the door. Business, have to be taken care of. If not I would definitely go for another round with you." Lola laughed. She heard the toilet flush. She grabbed a robe to head to the shower. She walked into the bathroom noticing a white powder lines on the counter. He took a hit. Lola gasped, embarrassed that she had no idea he used. "Um..."

"Oh shit, babe... I didn't know you were in here." He said with a smile. "You want a taste?" He replied. "No, that's okay." "You sure?" His eyes looked into hers concerned. "No. I'm good." She got in the shower as she heard him step out of the bathroom. She couldn't believe Vin used. He had been so attentive all the time, no signs of use. Everyone in entertainment had a candy of choice. But she didn't get that vibe with Vin. He was so tailored and spoke so well. His cufflinks always shining and she had never saw him in the same suit twice. She had a million thoughts rushing to her mind. She then thought about Dion again, guilt and shame filled her. Seconds later, Vin pulled back the curtain stepping in. "So, the driver will be here in about forty minutes. Is that enough time for you?" he said. "Yea, that's fine." Now with all the thoughts of Vin using in her mind, she felt awkward, she grabbed her robe to step out. Vin touched her arm. "Babe, I just use recreationally. I don't want you upset." He said sincerely.

"I'm fine." said Lola with a smile. She walked out to the closet. Thinking about the amazing sex they just had, she thought about King. She was going to see him again before they left. She put on a black strapless Herve dress with a pair of Chanel heels. She pinned her hair up in a bun, and began to reapply her makeup which was minimal. Her signature red lip, and light bronze on her cheeks. She heard the water stop and she walked over to the door. "Vin, I'm gonna go check on King."

"Alright."

She went down the hall towards their room. As she approached the door she saw a man walking towards their suite. He was wearing jeans, black tee, and fitted hat. She was curious what this person could want with Vin. He certainly didn't look like anyone Vin would associate with. She continued to stare at the man. He turned his head looking directly at her. She quickly turned back to the door, knocking softly. Soon, Vin's door opened and he stepped out in his pants and shirt unbuttoned. He and the man shook hands. Vin looked in her direction just as Janice opened the door and she quickly went in. "I'm so sorry miss, I was in the back and didn't hear over television. Hope you weren't out there long."

"It's okay. Where's King?" said Lola as she walked towards the bedroom. King was in the playpen, sleeping peacefully. Lola bent down picking him up. She kissed his lips as he moved away. He was a hard sleeper and moody like her when woken up. She smiled. "You want me to leave you alone." Said Lola as she kissed his head. Janice sat on the bed. Lola cuddled him a bit more. She laid him back in the playpen. He turned over ignoring her. "Well, tomorrow morning I will be busy. I would like to take him to the zoo, maybe Disney Land? Can you make those reservations, or at least for some time this week."

"Sure."

"Thank you. See you tomorrow. Bye luvie." Said Lola as she leaned in the playpen. Lola walked out of the door, as she made sure to close the door gently behind her. There was Vin in front of her face. "You ready?" Lola jumped startled. "Yes, I'm ready." He kissed her cheek taking her hand to escort her downstairs. "Oh, I need my purse." She replied. "You don't need it baby. I got you."

"No. I need my phone. Just in case something's up with my baby."

"Oh, I'm sorry." He opened the room for her to get her purse. He stood outside she saw her Chanel clutch beside the bed. She grabbed her phone seeing a box on the bed. She bent over the box trying to see what was inside. Vin cracked the door. "Ready babe?" He said.

Lola hurried towards the door as they were soon on their way to the party.

The party was a who's who of the Entertainment business. Champagne, cigars and power swirled the room. Lola had never seen a party like this before. Everything was gold, opulent, furs and extravagant. Sasha Money's music blared through the speakers.

"Fuck Love… roll me a dub. I'd rather fuck a boss for tha' paper, than be with a scrub!"

Vin began to shake everyone's hand and show off his beautiful lady. As they worked their way to an exclusive room, Lola eyes immediately went over to Sasha Money. She was even more stunning in person. She was wearing a Swarovski jeweled bra and matching shorts that fit like panties on her petite frame. "Vinny!" she yelled as she rushed over to him. She hugged him tight like a family member with slight passion as if he was an ex-lover she hadn't seen in forever.

"Hi, love. How are you?" Vin replied nonchalant. Lola stared at Sasha she didn't know if she should be pissed that she was on her man or in awe of her beauty. Sasha's skin was honey, she had almond shaped hazel eyes, with a piercing smile. Her hair ombre' platinum blonde and golden was curly and wild. She looked like a goddess as it cascaded over her shoulders. Most definitely a weave, but on her it didn't matter. She looked flawless.

"I'm good! I'm so happy to see you. She said in her West Indian accent. Who is this? Pretty girl."

"This is my lady, Lola." He kissed Lola's cheek.

"You are gorgeous! I am Sasha Money!" she said shaking her hand.

"Oh I know who you are. No intro needed at all. You're everywhere right now."

Sasha smiled. "This is true. I like you already. So, come over to my table. We have everything you need. Lola and Vin followed her over to the table. Rock should be back with the drop in a few minutes."

"Good."

Lola sat down and was immediately handed a glass of champagne. She looked at the table. Weed and pills littered the table. Lola sipped her drink. She looked to her right and three men were staring at her. Vin got up talking to people as they entered the room. One of the three men came over to her. Lola began to roll her eyes.

"Hi beautiful? You here alone?"

"No."

"Oh, okay. You into ménage?" He said with a smile on his face.

"Fuck you!" shouted Lola as she threw her drink in his face. She got up from the seat walking over to Vin across the room.

"That nigga over there just thought I was a fucking groupie!"

"What? Who?" said Vin angrily.

"Him! Lola pointed at the guy who was wearing a black jacket. He just asked me about a ménage!"

"Oh yeah. I'll handle it." Vin cuffed her face kissing her cheek again. He walked over towards the men. She looked over seeing him walk over to the man and whisper something in his ear. Minutes later he was walking back over to her. Everyone in the group scurried out of the area. Lola looked over at the guy he was slumped over in the seat.

"What did you do?" said Lola concerned.

"Nothing, baby. He won't be bothering you anymore." Said Vin kissing her lips. Two men walked over picking the guy up as Vin took Lola over to the others. Lola looked at Vin, was he really different than Uno? She began to contemplate if LA was a good idea. Vin began to introduce her to other friends. Lola smiled and mingled with everyone as her glass continued to be refilled. When a guy whispered to Vin that *"he's here."* He told Lola they were going to go to a backroom. As the guy approached them, he had a woman on his arms. She was dressed in an orange mini dress that showed off all of her curves, but she was thin, she looked famished. Lola realized it was Vita. She wanted to talk to her she looked stoned. Vin took Lola's hand again. "Come on baby, let's go in the back." The guy handed Vin's man a black handbag. He nodded and gave him a bag in return. Lola shook her head. *Were they really going to do a drug exchange in front of everyone?* Lola thought. Vita looked over at Lola. She smiled, admiring how flawless her little sister looked. Rock took her arm whisking her away. Lola not once looked back. They went in the back and his man opened the bag throwing the cocktail of drugs on the table.

Sasha came in a smile on her face. She immediately took to the cocaine. She picked up a pill throwing it in her mouth. She smiled as she wiped her nose. Lola looked at Vin she knew he was in heaven. He popped two pills and took to the cocaine. Lola sat watching these powerful people she had just admired get lost in the sea of drugs. She sat feeling uncomfortable as people in minutes began to feel the high of their choices. Sasha came over to Lola sitting on top of her lap. "Come on Lola! Have some fun, live a little!"

"No, I'm okay. You guys can enjoy." Said Lola with a smile. Sasha frowned. She put a pill in her mouth and then grabbed Lola's mouth kissing her. She tilted her head back, Lola pushed her away. "What are you doing?!" shouted Lola.

"Now you can live a little! Thank me later." said Sasha as she walked away. Soon blunts were passed around the room. Lola picked up a blunt taking a hit. She immediately began to cough hard, she felt as if she couldn't breathe. Vin came over to her, high as a kite. He took the blunt from her. "You okay baby?" He said with a smile. Lola finally came to. Vin took a hit of the blunt. The room began to spin around in Lola's head. She began to see pink and blue bears dancing on the table. She felt Vin's hands on her, as her skin felt like spiders were crawling on her. "Get them off me!" she began to shout.

"What, baby?" said Vin nonchalant.

"There is bugs all over me! Get them off!" she shouted. She saw Sasha in front of her face. She couldn't understand what she was saying, she poured something in Lola's mouth. "Here pretty, this will make you feel better."

The next day Lola awoke not remembering anything from last night. She looked around to see where she was. She was in the hotel's guest bathroom in the handicap stall. She tried to stand up, Vin was laying on her legs. She looked at her dress it was ripped down the middle and her breasts were exposed. Her jaw hurt and her leg was black and blue. She hit Vin. "Get up!" He didn't budge. She walked over to the sink, stumbling. She saw her face in the mirror. Her makeup was smeared, her hair a mess. She wet her face then went over to Vin again. She kicked him. He moaned. "What the fuck?" he mumbled. She looked at her heels, they were broken she took them off. She kicked him again. "Get up!" Vin moaned again opening his eyes. "Where the fuck are we?" He said looking around the room. He saw they were in the bathroom. He smiled. "You okay?" he said to Lola.

"No! I don't remember anything! I have a son!" she replied.

Vin got off the floor. He looked at her sympathetically. "I'm sorry. I thought you were enjoying yourself. You were so nervous earlier that night, thought you decided to take edge off."

"No, Sasha I think drugged me!" said Lola. Vin went over to the toilet relieving his self. Lola shook her head. "I'm out of here." She unlocked the stall door walking out. There was a man using the urinal in front. He smiled. "Hey." Lola looked down realizing her breasts were exposed. She grabbed her dress trying to close it. Vin came out the stall. "Baby... wait!" he shouted. He saw the guy looking at Lola's body. "The fuck you looking at, huh?" the guy finished up leaving the bathroom without washing his hands. Vin walked over to the door locking it.

"Listen, I'm sorry. Don't fucking leave." He began to take off his shirt. "What are you doing?" she replied.

"Here, put this on." She put the shirt on buttoning up the top buttons. Vin then kissed her face. "I'm going to make this up to you. Okay, I promise." She looked into his eyes. He looked genuine. She left out the bathroom he followed behind her. Men stood outside the door looking at them. Lola couldn't help but smile at how ridiculous she looked. Vin looked at her. "Fuck them. You're beautiful, you hear me." He kissed her cheek again. They went up to the room. Lola went straight for the shower. She was not going to let King see her like this. Vin followed behind. She locked the door behind her. Vin came to the door turning the knob realizing he was locked out. He left the door.

Lola stayed in the shower for over twenty minutes. When she stepped out she put her robe on placing a towel around her wet hair. She unlocked the door walking out, there was roses everywhere surrounding the room. There was a life size stuffed bear in the center with an *"I'm Sorry"* balloon. This scene had seemed dejavu to her. She moved the roses walking over to the bed. There was three tickets and a piece of paper. It said "Enjoy Disneyland with King & Janice. I'm going to clean myself up. I'm sorry, I let you down." She put the letter back down and walked over to the closet. The floor was lined with: Louis Vuitton, Chanel, Dior, Valentino, Christian Louboutin and Giuseppe Zanotti. She smiled looking through all the bags. Today was going to be a good day. She called up Vita to invite her then she thought about Vin last night. Vita was her best friend, but she couldn't have King around that. She hung up before it went to voicemail. She changed into her clothes and headed down to their suite.

Opportunities and Agendas

A month and a half later, Lola threw King a birthday party at the park. With all of the girls from the club and their kids in attendance.. He had a two tier cake with a football and Dion's family came to attend. Lola hired a professional photographer and the whole picnic table was covered in gifts. King was to go back to Pennsylvania with the family today. She was sad to see her little man go. But, he needed to be around his father's family. Julia and David, Dion's parents were on their way to pick up King. Lola had packed up his bags and had them waiting by the door. Lola sat on the couch kissing King. He would be gone until the middle of September. This was the longest he would be away from her. The doorbell rang and she got up with King to answer. David picked up King. Lola hugged them both.

"We're so excited to have him. We've fixed up the spare room, and Mama can't wait to see him." said Julia. King began to cry. David smiled.

"Oh, you don't want grandpa." Said Lola as she kissed his cheek. Julia took him out of David's arms. He continued to cry, his cries getting louder. Julia began to rock him gently. He whined his face turning red. Lola picked him up. He quieted down, looking into his mommy's face. "Oh, no King's a Mommy's Boy." Said David as he picked up his luggage. Lola began to rock him, kissing his forehead. "He will be fine." said Lola reassuringly. Not sure if she was trying to convince herself or them.

"Well, we better be going if we want to be on time for this flight." Said David as he walked inside again. Lola grabbed King's carrier. She felt he knew he was leaving her. He clamped on to her shirt, his face buried in her neck. Lola couldn't help herself, she began to cry. She kissed his cheek, caressing his back.

"So, you guys will call me every day right? I will come on September fifteenth to pick him up. Maybe a few days before to be safe." Said Lola wiping back her tears.

"Certainly. We will call every day and maybe we can video chat or something like that." said Julia. Julia stretched her arms to take King. Lola didn't want to let him go, but she knew that being around his family would be good for him. She kissed him once more. "I love you more than anything luvie." She said as she handed him to Julia. Julia and David smiled looking onward to their exchange. King smiled at his Mommy as Julia took him in her arms. David came over hugging her again.

"So we will see you soon." Said David.

Lola couldn't compose herself. "Okay, guys... call me when you arrive home. I can't right now. Please. Take care of my baby."

"We will, Lauren." Said David. As he took the carrier in his hand. Julia walked out of the door with King. He began to cry as she walked out the door. David walked out of the door. Lola locked it behind them, falling dramatically behind it, as tears fell from her face. Hours later she was in the same spot, behind the door. Her phone rang it was Julia stating that they were on their way home and King was asleep. Lola felt a little better she replied okay, thank you. She looked at the clock on her phone it was almost time for her to get ready for the club. She took a shower, afterward throwing on tights and white v-neck tee. As she got in her car pulling out the driveway she received a call, it was a New York area code. She froze up. She answered the call.

"Hello." She said nastily.

"Hi, Lola? It's me, Sasha Money. Are you busy?"

Lola looked at the phone, wondering was this true and how did she get her number.

"I'm on my way to work. Why?"

"Yes, I heard about the work you do. I don't think that's a good job for someone gorgeous as you. I think you should come on tour with me, I have a few sexy sets I need gorgeous girls. I can guarantee you will make three times as much as you make in Vegas."

"I'm not really interested in that lifestyle." Said Lola bluntly.

"What lifestyle? Getting money?" Sasha replied.

"No thank you. I know what you did at the party and the balls of you to fuckin' call me after that shit baffles me."

"It was a party. That's what we do. I'm sorry if it offended you, but you don't have to be nasty about it."

"Bitch, don't tell me how to react I have a son! I can't be out here reckless, you understand! So, I don't give a fuck how you feel!" said Lola fuming.

"See, you don't get it. Vegas is not forever, I'm trying to help you, you don't want my help...fine." said Sasha. She hung up the phone. Lola looked at the phone. Call Ended. "No she fucking didn't." she threw the phone in the seat. After work that night she brought home about five grand. She and the girls went out for breakfast and Maitai told her that she and Butterscotch were approached by people for Sasha Money and were going to go on tour with her.

"Yea, it's paying fifteen thousand a show." Said Maitai.

"I mean that's not crazy paper, but the exposure... shit could lead to more." Said Butterscotch.

"What about y'all kids? I mean you're gonna leave your kids for fifteen g's." said Lola.

"I've been working clubs here, a long time. I've seen bitches come in and let Vegas chew them up and spit them out. I'm ready to start a future for my kids and a decent living. I don't want to be a fucking stripper forever." Said Butterscotch as she looked away. Lola hadn't thought about it that way, what was her future after dancing.

After breakfast, she decided to call Sasha Money back about the opportunity. The phone rang three times.

"Hello." Said Lola.

"I knew you would call back. So, you thought about my offer eh?"

"Yea, I spoke to my girls who said you reached out to them too. They said it was paying fifteen grand a show. I consider that a pay decrease, I can stay at the club for that."

"I didn't say, you would be making fifteen grand a show. How about thirty grand a show?" Lola almost spit out her drink. She regained her composure.

"How many shows?"

"Honey, I'm going on a world tour over a hundred cities, four continents. I'm not aware on all my details yet, that's what I have a staff for. I will have them email info to you. We are meeting in California for rehearsals and all that shit in about two weeks. Anyway, that will be given to you. So, I take that as a yes?"

"I don't know yet. Send me info and I'll think about it."

                    *   *   *

Two weeks later and Lola hadn't heard from Julia and David about King. She had become worried thinking something had happened. She tried to remain calm by telling herself that maybe they had went out of town to visit family, she remembered Dion told her they had family in New York, maybe they went on vacation. Sasha's team had sent over contract and today was the last day for her decision. She pulled out her cellphone to call Julia. She walked out to the patio, sitting on a bench. "*The number you have reached has been disconnected. Please try again."* She hung up the phone. Her blood pressure beginning to boil. She called David's number. A disconnected beep began to rang through the speaker. Lola got up. *"I know, this is not happening."* She went into the house looking through her things looking for an address book. She found Destiny's phone number. She called her number it rang two times and went to voice mail. Lola became furious. She began packing up a bag. Her cell rang again she looked at the screen. It was Vin.

"Hello." She replied frantically.

"Hey, baby. What's wrong?" said Vin.

"I've been calling King's grandparents and all their numbers are disconnected. I believe they have kidnapped my baby!" she shouted.

"Calm down, baby. I'm on the way."

"No. it's okay, I'm on my way to Pennsylvania."

"Lola, wait. I'll go with you." He said reassuringly. She hung up the phone. Lola began pacing around. She called their number again. No response. She called Paul's number. It rang three times and someone answered.

"Hello." He said half groggy.

"Hey, this is Lola. I've been calling your parents to check on King, and their numbers are off. What's going on?" she said angrily.

"I don't know, about their phones. But, I saw King last night, they were supposed to go visit the family in New York today." He replied nonchalant.

"They haven't said anything to me in two weeks. I think I deserve to know what the fuck is going on with my son!" said Lola.

"Well, did it ever occur to you that they deserve to know what happened to theirs?"

"What are you talking about?"

"We saw the police reports; you had no information on anything. You made sure you got your money off my brother every month. You left the place in Cali, bare."

"What the fuck are you trying to say? You don't fucking know me."

"Oh, I know a little about you Lola and your career in Vegas."

"Look, you coward motherfucka... I want my son. If you bastards think y'all are gonna keep him from me, you've got me fucked up! Bring me my child."

"Is that a threat?"

"Call it whatever the fuck you want!" she shouted.

"I told Dion when he wanted to marry you, something wasn't right about you. You were always secretive, did your best to keep him away from his family."

"Fuck you! I loved Dion, I would've gave my life for him." she shouted as tears streamed down her cheeks.

"No, he just gave up his for you. Ever since you came into Dion's life you fucked everything up. I know you are the reason for his murder! I'm going to get to the bottom of it!" Paul hung up the phone. Lola began to cry. She thought about the day Dion was shot and all the emotions that came during that period in her life. Her doorbell rang she rushed over to the door. She didn't look in the peephole. She opened the door, it was a guy in all black, with a box in his hand. "Who are you?"

"Just delivering a package to you."

The guy walked back to the black suburban driving away. Lola opened the box. Inside it was filled with pictures. She looked through them; they were of King and his grandparents. Pictures of her picking him up from school. One of the last pictures was of King sleeping in a bed. *"You don't want him to be touched like his father do you? Call this number by midnight."* Lola knew it could only be Uno. She panicked deciding to call the only person who could help her in this situation would be Vita.

Her phone rang three times.

"Hello." Said Vita.

"Hey... I just received this box, I think from Uno, he's been watching me and King. I think he's going to do something to him. I don't know what to do?"

"What?! What'd it say?"

"It was pictures of King, and it said don't let him end up like his father. I have to call a number by midnight. King's people aren't answering the phone; I don't know what to do." Said Lola her voice becoming weak.

"Shit... call the number, and see what's up. Maybe can trace it back to someone." She replied. Lola wrote the number down. Just calm down and call the number call me back once you find out something.

"Okay."

She called the number it rang once.

"I figured, you would call, said the voice. So, this is what's going to happen? You are going to drop off one-hundred thousand dollars to the Hilton. If you look in the bottom of the box there should be a room key. Leave the money in the room, and we won't touch your boy."

"Wait, but I don't have that type of money."

"Stop fucking lying! You want to see your son, bring it by tonight. Room 223." The phone hung up. Lola sat confused. The doorbell rang she looked through the peephole. It was Vin. She opened the door hugging him. He kissed her cheek. "Now, what's going on?" he walked behind her over to the couch. She began to fill him in on what happened. But, as she told him the story again, it began to not make any sense. Why would Uno want money from her? Was it all a set up to get her to come to the location? Uno would want her so he could beat her and possibly rape her. But sending him money, he wouldn't do.

"So, this is what we will do: I will give you the money to put in the bag. We will have one of the dancers to put the money in the room. You go on that tour with Sasha Money. I think they will be flying to Atlanta for rehearsals and then heading for New York. I will meet you in New York, and I will have got a location on King. You will have to take him on the road with you, as well as me."

"You're going too?" said Lola.

"I can't have anything happen to you. When you come back you leave this house we find you a new one, in a different state. I'll handle this for you. Don't you worry your pretty head, okay?" He kissed her lips. She would be putting a lot of trust in Vin.

"Do you have a passport?" said Vin.

"Yea, but King"

"We'll, handle that."

By five that afternoon, she was on a plane with Sasha Money's camp heading to Atlanta. Lola felt some type of way having him handle this situation, but she couldn't be too relaxed in her old stomping grounds. Once settled in their room they were to be at rehearsal for four hours and into the night. Lola was not in the mood. Three hours into rehearsal, her phone vibrated, it said *"come to the hotel ASAP."* Lola spoke to the choreographer and asked if she could leave early. After promising to stay later next rehearsal she was allowed to leave. She threw on her shades, taking a taxi to the hotel. She rushed up to the room. "Vin? Vin?" she dropped her bag walking over to the couches. There he was with King in hand, sleeping. Lola let out a cry. "My baby!" She ran over to him, picking up King she kissed his lips cradling him in her arms. "My luvie! I love you soo much!" she replied as her tears fell on his face. She looked at Vin. "Thank you! Thank you, baby. How can I ever, repay you for what you've done?" She kissed his lips.

"I don't ever want anything from you Lola, but your love. Say you will always be there for me." He said with sincere eyes. Lola kissed his lips. "I'll always be there for you." He handed her a passport book. She opened it, it was for King. "Oh, thank you... so much!" Lola wiped her eyes.

"Janice, will be here soon. She'll be going on the road with us, to watch King. See, I have everything taken care of baby." She loved the way he had taken care of the situation. She really didn't want details on how or what, all she cared was that she had her baby and he was safe. She felt turned on by his bravado. She walked over to the crib, placing King inside. She walked back over to Vin kissing his lips. She had to have him now. He threw her onto the bed and in seconds their bodies were making sweet sounds in the moonlight.

After two rounds, Vin got up and said he had to make some final business plans before they leave the country. Lola looked at his body, his chiseled pecs, and his dick that swayed from side to side. She began to think how much Vin had grown on her. She thought of how they had never argued or had any ill feelings towards each other, since they met. She wrapped a robe around her body and went to check on King. He was still sleeping. She walked over to the bathroom door. She gently opened it, preparing to surprise him. She saw the lines he had made on the counter. He cleared two as he prepared for the third. He looked towards the door. Lola closed the door walking out. Janice came an hour later and said she was excited about visiting the different countries. King had awoke excited to see his mommy. Lola ordered him food from room service. She gave Janice some money to go buy food for him for the next day. Vin had already left. Lola began to think about Nana Anna. She wanted to see her. After Janice came back, Lola took a car service to Jacksonville, she had to see her.

As she rode by seeing all the places she used to rob and a few people she had issues with and fought, she felt nostalgic. She wondered what Nana was doing. Was she okay? Was she eating? She missed her so. She told the driver to pull on the back street of the house. She was wearing jeans and an YSL shirt, Timberland boots. She jumped the fence. She went around to the basement window, which she used to sneak in thru after late night. It was still unlocked. She opened the window slowly, shimmying her way in. she walked up the steps the floorboards creaking as she walked. "Shit." She mumbled. She opened the door looking at the kitchen; everything was exactly how she remembered. She walked around to the living room, she crept up the stairs. She walked towards Anna's room, the door was cracked. Lola pushed open the door softly.

"Is that my Lola?"

Lola flipped the light switch which was on the wall. In the light everything became clear, the room was a mess and Anna was lying in bed the room reeked of urine. Lola began to cry.

"It's me Nana. I'm so sorry." Lola walked over to her bed lying on her chest. Anna moved slowly trying to touch her face. Lola felt her body she was very frail. Lola kissed her face. "What happened? When was the last time you ate? Left this room?"

"No one has been by this week. The church is going through some things. I'll be okay. She touched Lola's face. Look, at you, you look like a beautiful girl, I always knew you were."

Lola blushed. "Can you walk Nana?"

"Not too good by myself." Anna stared at Lola in amazement as she attempted to help her from the bed.

"We're going to get you in the bath and you can tell me all about what's been going on." Once in the tub, Lola could see that she hadn't bathed in a while. It broke her heart to see her this way. She told the car service to pull around front and she brought groceries inside. She brought Nana downstairs and cooked her dinner. She made her Baked Chicken and pasta. Anna ate every bit as Lola watched her.

"You have a grandson." Said Lola

"I do?"

"Yea, his name is King. Lola pulled out her phone and showed her a picture of him.

"He's handsome. He looks just like you did at that age." Lola smiled as Nana kissed her forehead. "I'm going to arrange to have a nurse come here every day. I don't want to ever find you like this again."

"Where are you now?" said Anna.

"I'm in Vegas."

Anna nodded her head. "I've been worried about you. I pray for you every day and I knew eventually God would bring you back to me. Are you okay my child?"

"I'm good. I've taken good care of myself, and provide a good home for me and my son. Eventually, I want you to live with us. So I can make sure you're taken care of."

"Baby, I will always be fine. I'll always be right here. That food was good. Oh, yeah look on the table next to the door; those were some letters up there for you."

"From who?"

"Prison… I believe." Lola walked over to the table getting the letters. She looked at the name Rico Bailey. She felt sick. There was two whole stacks of letters. Lola threw them in her bag. "Did you want to open it?"

"No… that's okay. Let's get you some water and I'll change your sheets and flip your bed." She went upstairs picking up her Nana's room once she was finished she came down to help her upstairs. She tucked her in bed. "I'm going to come back for you Nana. I love you so much. She kissed her face again. Don't forget I'm going to have a nurse come by. She looked at her phone it displayed four am. I have to go." Anna smiled at her.

"I will be fine. I love you too. Remember you don't have to take on the world alone. Let, someone love you baby. Don't be afraid of love." Said Anna. Lola smiled looking at her. She hugged her once more before leaving the room. She went into her room she saw her letter from her basket taped on the mirror she took it off gently, placing it in her bag. She looked around her small space that used to be her everything. She smiled walking out. "Remember Lola, the battle is not yours..." "I know, it's the Lord's... I love you." Lola went back out the way she came in. She smiled looking back on her old house.

The next day was hectic everyone was running around trying to get last minute things together and rehearsals. Sasha had interviews and press all morning. She asked Lola to ride with her to interviews. She took a few pills to take the edge off. She offered Lola some she shook her head no. Lola was on the phone setting up a nurse to come to check on Nana, as well as meal delivery service. King was at the room with Janice, everything was falling into place.

<u>Backstage Pass</u>

"1...2...3...and 4. Sexy. Sexy. Shy." Shouted Eve the choreographer. The rehearsals were brutal. Some days nine hours, nonstop in heels, and on their knees. Butterscotch had enough, she sat on the floor catching her breath. "Are you tired, honey? Get your ass up and let's work!" Eve taunted thrusting her hips from side to side. Butterscotch rolled her eyes. Lola saw the look on her face she knew Eve was working her nerves today. Maitai winked at her, signaling her not to lose her cool. After rehearsal, that night everyone was going out to dinner. Lola was not sure yet if she was going to go. Since they arrived in London she had not yet spent time with King or Vin. She figured today they could all go sightseeing. She was feeling good, she decided to call Janice. She realized her phone was missing. Once she arrived at the hotel room King was on the floor playing with his blocks. "Hi luvie!" she picked him up and he began to smile as she threw him in the air. He giggled loudly. Janice walked over. "Hi miss."

"Hi, Janice. Have you seen my phone?"

"No. I haven't seen it. Mr. Vin said he would like to see you."

"He's here?"

"No, he's at your suite." Said Janice.

"Okay. I'll be right back." Said Lola. She handed King over to Janice. "Can you get him dressed were going out when I come back. She walked next door to the suite, Vin was sitting at the table. "Hey, how was rehearsal?" He got up kissing her cheek. "It was okay. I'm tired. I want to go sightseeing. Have you seen my phone? Now that I think about it I haven't seen it, since Atlanta."

Vin looked down at his hands. "I got rid of it."

"What?" said Lola.

"Yea, you didn't need that trail. So, I got rid of it." Said Vin nonchalant.

"What trail? What do you mean?"

"Well, it's nothing to worry your pretty head about. King is safe." He got up walking to the mirror.

"What did you do?!" she shouted.

"Calm down. Okay, they are fine. They won't be bothering you and King anymore."

"You killed them?"

"No." He said genuinely. Lola looked into his eyes.

"I don't like anyone keeping secrets from me. Especially if it involves my son."

"Lola, I love you. I've been nothing but honest with you since we've been together. They are alive. I can assure you." He came back over to her. He began to kiss her neck. "What am I to do about a phone? I need a phone."

"I can handle that for you."

"What about your business in Vegas, how are you gonna keep up with that on tour?"

"You trying to get rid of me? My business is mobile I don't have to be in Vegas. Besides, I thought this would be a good time for us to be together, get to know each other better." He kissed her lips. He smelled so good, his touch strong yet gentle is what Lola began to love about him. But there was always some mystery behind him. Did he have family? Did he have a criminal past? She pulled away from him, we definitely need to get to know each other. She said seriously. "Ask Away..." He sat on the couch sitting her on his lap. An hour she learned that Vincent Nariela, was born in Italy, raised in Chicago. His family was part of one of Chicago's biggest Crime families. He had one sibling a younger sister. His father was killed in a drive by with a rival family, left him riddled with twelve holes. His mother distraught and disheartened by the incident moved them to California, Where they started a new life. Lola was shocked.

"So what happened? Are you still connected?"

Vin looked away. "No, I'm not involved in that. That was my father's life."

"What about your mom?"

"She's in Florence."

"So is that why you wanted to come on tour?"

"I can always come to Florence, whenever I want. I wanted to spend time with you." He smiled at her. Lola kissed his cheek. She was happy they had this talk, but she still thought there was more.

They went out sight-seeing, snapping pictures Vin had a photographer follow them as they picked up souvenirs. Hours later when they came back King was sleeping. She put him to bed, and headed back to their suite. When she opened the door she saw Vin snorting lines again. He looked as though he was going to fall over. She rushed over to him.

"Why do you do this shit?!" she shouted.

He looked at her his eyes wide. "Baby its nothing. Really, I'll be fine."

"I didn't ask you that, I said why."

"I need it." He said compassionately. She looked away from him, becoming lost in her own thoughts. She went towards the bathroom. Vin came over to her. "Why do you look at me like that, when I use? It feels like you're looking down on me."

"Vin, I've told you I don't like it."

"No, you just pop pills." Said Vin.

"What?!"

"You heard me! I know you pop fucking pills, Lola."

"And I know that story you told me is a crock of shit! You're still involved." Vin grabbed her arm.

"And if I'm still involved. So what?" said Vin defensively.

"You're high. Get the fuck off me." She pushed him away. She looked over and saw his stash of coke sitting on the couch. She rushed towards it. He followed after her as she grabbed it in her hands. He tackled her to the floor. "Don't play with me Lola. After all the shit I just did for you." Lola thought about King she let go of the bag. He grabbed it, placing it in his pocket. Lola stood up.

"I can't have King exposed to all of this. Do you understand?" she replied sternly. She stormed out of the room downstairs to the lobby. When she arrived in the lobby she realized that a crowd was forming outside. Paparazzi and cameras begin to flash as Sasha came strutting into the lobby.

"Lola!" shouted Sasha.

"Hi. How are you?" said Lola.

"I'm fabulous honey. Why don't you bring your gorgeous self to my party tonight?"

"Where? We have an early morning tomorrow." Said Lola unsure if a late night would be in her best interest, furthermore this was her boss.

"Fuck tomorrow. You're my best dancer anyway, you will be great."

Sasha put her arms around Lola escorting her up to her room as paparazzi snapped pictures. Sasha's room was gorgeous. Everything was white, elegant and expensive clothing bags lined the floor. "Everyone get the fuck out!" Sasha barked to her glam team as they prepared her look for tonight. Lola walked towards the door. "Where are you going? I meant those bitches need to get out." She sat on the bed, pulling out a blunt. Sasha was so beautiful and cool. Although, she was the number one artist in the world, Lola loved the fact she seemed so down to earth. Sasha took a few pulls of the blunt looking into Lola's eyes.

"What do you want after all this?" she replied seriously.

"I've never quite thought about that. To provide for my son, and hopefully get off the pole." Lola said with a smile.

Sasha passed the blunt to Lola. Lola took a hit, it was strong. She began to cough. Sasha smiled getting off the bed. "You have something love. I've seen a lot of these bitches, get in the industry and stay until there pussy has been ran thru by any and everybody. You stay in long enough to make your connections. Use this shit as a platform to becoming your own boss feel me. Just get the fuck out while you can." Lola nodded her head thinking about what Sasha said, she had never thought about it. What would she do after this tour? Sasha picked up her dress they had left for her to wear. She threw it. "I'm not wearing that shit!" Lola put down the blunt looking at the dress that she'd thrown, it was a sequin strapless dress that was gorgeous. But, she wasn't going to question Sasha. Sasha came out the closet naked, she asked Lola to try it on. "I don't think it will fit me. You're smaller than me." "Nonsense. I think it will look better on you." Lola looked up at Sasha's body, she was tiny. Lola took off her clothes sliding the dress on. Sasha walked over to her she placed her hands on Lola's hips. "It looks fabulous on you." She ran her fingers through her hair teasing out her hair. "Give you a nude lip gloss, lashes. I'm gonna make you a star." She smiled cuffing her hand around Lola's chin.

"Makeup Now!" Screamed Sasha. Her staff hurried into the room running to her side. Lola looked at herself in the mirror. "Do Lola's makeup, I want something else fabulous. Now!" Sasha's glam squad rushed over to Lola starting on her face. "Would you like some wine love?" said Sasha.

"Okay." Said Lola.

"Bring us the best wine they have here, immediately. Go!" She yelled to her assistant. She hurried out of the room. Lola looked around in awe at everyone scurrying around. An hour later they were glam and ready to go, Sasha threw a pair of shades on her face. As they took the elevator, downstairs Lola felt a buzz. Sasha smiled at her opening her hand revealing a few pills. "They'll take the edge off." Lola looked at them, they looked like the ones she had always taken. Sasha took two of them in her mouth, Lola took the last ones and put them in her mouth. "Bottoms up, sexy. Welcome to the good life." said Sasha. The room began to spin, Lola held on to the elevator wall.

Two weeks had passed Lola had been out with Sasha every night. She hadn't spent over an hour with King. Vin hadn't been able to get her alone since the first night they went out. Sasha was making Lola a star, people wanted to know who was the "hottie" on her arm, but Sasha kept them at bay, she loved to keep them guessing, keeping her eyes and head covered at all times. They were in Amsterdam for two days, they had rehearsals, but Sasha told Lola she didn't have to go to rehearsals. They were going shopping. They were in Sasha's Mercedes going to a boutique.

"Eventually I'm gonna have to go to rehearsals. Everyone is going to hate me." Said Lola.

"Who gives a fuck what those bitches think? I am the boss, I choose who I want to do what. They don't like it, they can be replaced." Sasha looked through her purse, "I need some fucking blow."

Lola looked over at her surprised. They popped pills and smoked plenty of blunts in one day. But she was shocked that Sasha did blow. Lola looked at her as she scurried through her bag. They had popped a few pills that morning. Sasha found some in her satchel, she smiled. She pulled out her wallet and titanium American Express card, as she made a line. She rolled up a hundred dollar bill.

"Lo, you want some?"

"No, I'm okay."

Sasha took two lines. Lola looked out the window not wanting to stare at her while she topped herself off. Lola got deep into her thoughts about the last few weeks, and Dion. She always thought about him when she got depressed. She felt two hands on her inner thigh. Lola turned around startled, not knowing how to react. Sasha smiled lifting Lola's dress. Lola pulled her dress down. "Sasha... you're high."

"No, I've wanted you for a long time now. She closed the privacy blind so the driver couldn't listen. Since the day I met you. She began to kiss Lola's neck and ear. Lola was so confused, she thought they had a good friendship. Sasha got on top of Lola's lap, she began to kiss her lips. Lola could taste the cocaine on her lips. She tried to pull away from Sasha as she grabbed her face sternly, forcing her tongue down her throat. She ripped off the top of Lola's dress, which was strapless and she had no bra on. Sasha began to suck on her breasts while placing her fingers into Lola's panties. Lola let out a moan as her finger made contact with her clit. Lola didn't want to admit she liked it. She began to kiss Sasha's lips passionately, she ripped off Sasha's top. She smiled in delight as Lola began to suck her breast. Sasha grabbed some of the line that was left on the card placing it on her finger sticking it in Lola's mouth.

Sasha went to her knees parting Lola's legs open. Her panties at this point were drenched. Sasha took out her blade and cut Lola's panties off. She began to kiss Lola's inner thighs playing gently with her pussy with her fingers. Lola grabbed on to door panel, squirming in ecstasy.

"Oh..." she let out finally. Sasha smiled as she placed her tongue inside her walls. She gently poked her with her stiletto gel fingers. Lola began to feel the coke set in. Sasha reached into her Louis Vuitton bag on the floor, she pulled out a 10" dildo. She smiled at Lola, as she gently slid it in her vagina. Lola began to scream out; Sasha went deeper, spreading her leg in the air her foot touching the car ceiling. As she went harder Lola clutched the leather seat. Lola sat up grabbing the dildo out of her vagina, she licked it clean. She grabbed Sasha by her throat pinning her to the seat.

"Fuck me." Said Sasha pleading. Lola opened Sasha's legs, ripping off her panties. Letting her tongue dance in Sasha's sugar walls, then ramming the dildo inside of her. A two sided dildo Lola sat on top of it riding

Sasha as they both went to ecstasy. Lola blacked out. When she awoke, she looked around the dark room trying to figure out where she was.

She was in Sasha's suite. Naked. She sat up in the bed looking around for Sasha. She got up placing the sheet over herself. She felt like she wanted to vomit. Sasha came from the bathroom, naked a smile on her face. "Hi, love." Lola looked at her naked body, in the light she was gorgeous. She had diamonds tattooed on the side of her vagina. Her perky breasts and soft silky skin aroused Lola. Sasha walked over to Lola, sitting on top of her lap. "What happened here?"

"We fucked... over and over again."

"What?"

"Don't act like you don't remember."

"I remember we were to go shopping and we fucked in the car right?'

"That was four days ago, baby. We've been fucking every day since then. Almost every hour? You've had a few qualos, babe. Were in Australia now. Your baby is down the hall with the nanny, they are fine." Sasha ran her fingers through Lola's hair, she kissed Lola's lips slowly. Sasha reached over on the nightstand her mirror with her lines already made. She did two wiping her nose, she handed it to Lola. "You're gonna need it before you crash, baby." Lola did one line, as Sasha spread her legs open. Her head began to spin.

Weeks went by Lola didn't remember anything. By the time they reached the Caribbean, Lola was an addict.

She hadn't seen Vin since their argument but knew he was still around. Everyone knew that Lola was Sasha's lover, and she made no point to hide it. On stage in Africa, Lola had felt a hundred roaches were on her and made a mockery of the show. But, because Sasha loved her she wasn't penalized. She hadn't performed on stage since Africa. Sasha was her provider and everything. Every day she woke up to fuck Sasha and have more blow. Lola had begun stealing stacks of money from Sasha's bags, hiding them inside of her luggage each time she came back to reality. She hadn't eaten in days and her weight began to wither.

She woke up naked like always and realized she was in her own suite. She went to the bathroom. She looked at herself in the mirror, washing her face. She stared at her reflection in the mirror. She had scratches on her arms and bruises on her thighs. Where she didn't remember where they came from. There was a knock at the door, her head was spinning. She walked over to the door naked. "What!" she yelled as she opened the door. He stood there appalled. "Lola, what's happened to you babe?" said Vin stepping into the room covering her body.

"What do you mean, what's wrong with me?" She threw her hands in the air walking towards the bed. "When's the last time you saw King? Janice?"

"They are fine."

Lola pulled out her purse dumping it on the bed. She began to search it frantically. Vin shook his head. "You were the one always yelling at me about my shit and look at you. What's happened to you?"

"I'm fucking fine. She began to throw her empty pill bottles across the room. Do you have any blow?" said Lola her lips began to chatter.

"No."

"Yes, you do. I know you do." She got up from the bed walking over to Vin. She began to kiss on his neck.

"What are you doing, Lola?" She wrapped her leg around his body; she threw him to the bed. She ripped off his clothes, revealing his dick. "I'll fuck you so good, you won't remember today. If you give me some blow." She began to kiss his dick slowly; he began to squirm, as she deep throated his shaft.

"Oh what the hell" He reached into his pocket and handed Lola the drugs. Lola smiled, throwing it on her bedside mirror making a few lines. She took all three before climbing on top of Vin. When she awoke Vin's face was buried in her neck and his dick was still in side of her, it was the next day. She tried to move him off and he began fucking her again. She began to scream out. He got up holding her head up against the board, kissing her ear. "Oh, shit… you feel fucking good." He shouted. The door opened in walked Sasha, in her trench coat. "How could you do this to me Lola!" She screamed throwing her purse at them. Vin hopped off of Lola. "Sasha, what is wrong with you?" Sasha threw off her trench coat revealing her naked body. Vin stared at her in amazement. She slapped Vin's face walking over towards Lola. They embraced kissing each other's lips.

"What the fuck is wrong with you Sasha she was my bitch first!"

"You can't fuck her like I can." She threw Lola on the bed; she began to kiss her slowly. Lola grabbed her ass as Sasha sat on top of her. "We'll see about that." Vin climbed on the bed. He pulled Lola down to him as Sasha remained on her stomach. Lola grabbed a handful of pills off her nightstand, as Vin slid his dick back inside of her. Sasha angry sat on Lola's face, bouncing up and down as Lola licked every ounce of her box dry. Soon, Vin was fucking Sasha while she fucked Lola with the dildo. Then Sasha sat on Vin's face and Lola rode him, and lastily Sasha lay on the bottom and Lola lay half lifeless on top of her, Vin began to fuck both of their holes. Sasha began to scream out in agony as Lola turned over and placed the dildo in her ass as Vin fucked Sasha's pussy. Sasha began to scream louder Lola went deeper and deeper. Lola then took the dildo out of her ass and stuck it in her mouth. Sasha began to gag as Lola pushed it further down her throat. Vomit spewed from her mouth unto Lola's face. Lola laughed loudly and menacingly.

Lola took the dick out slapping Sasha across the face. "Can't handle it!" Vin pulled Lola on top of him as they finished each other off. Sasha lay in her vomit, Vin and Lola lay on the floor her pussy on his face. Sasha got up showered and dressed she looked at them out cold, she kicked them. "You're both fucking fired! Lola you fuckin cheated on me, you're done here!" Sasha grabbed Lola by the hair pulling her off Vin. Lola began to fight her back, look at you! Shouted Sasha, pathetic. You chose this crack head over me, I made you a star."

"Fuck you Sasha." Lola ripped Sasha's bag off her shoulder. They began to fight as Lola went thru stealing her cash and pills. Sasha slapped her, Lola threw Sasha's passport and cards at Sasha's face. "Get the fuck out bitch!

You don't know me! I will blow your fuckin brains out!" shouted Lola as she searched the room for Vin's gun. Sasha panicked grabbing her cell phone on the floor. Quickly dialed her security as Lola rushed into the bathroom. Minutes later, Sasha's security came thru the room doors escorting Sasha out, searching the room for Lola who was tapped out on the bathroom floor.

Lauren

Lola woke up in a white room, with cinderblock walls. She looked down at her body seeing she was wearing a hospital gown. She felt horrible all over. She then looked around for her belongings and saw nothing she then thought of King.

"Where is my baby? Where is my fucking son?" She screamed out loud. A nurse came into the room, wearing white scrubs, mid-forties, black with a short haircut. She looked over at Lola, her eyes concerned yet judgmental.

"Do you know where you are?"

"Where is my child?" she barked back as she tried to remove herself from the bed. She looked down at the IV's in her arm ripping them out of her arm. The nurse folded her arms looking over at her.

"So, what you're supposed to be mad now huh? If you were so concerned about that baby, you wouldn't be doing what you're doing to yourself. How are you gonna take care of a baby, when you're dead?"

The woman's words stung like a bullet to her heart. *Who was this bitch?* She didn't know her life, she didn't know the things she had been through, what gave her the right to talk to her like that. Lola looked over at the woman sneering, everything in her wanted to get up and beat the shit out of her.

"If you're done with your little tirade, you are in Malibu, California. You are at a rehab facility; you need to use this time to figure out what's important in your life. From what I've heard your child is with your sister."

"Wait... Y'all can't do this shit! I did not sign up for this. I am not staying here!"

"They've had to pump your stomach numerous times, you fell into a stupor and have been here about two weeks now. You are staying here for three months."

"Fuck you! I'm not staying here!" Lola grabbed a cup of water from the table throwing it at the woman. The lady smirked moving out the way. "You young bitches, can have everything but choose to throw it all away. She shook her head as she walked over towards Lola. Two guards came in to try to restrain Lola as the woman stuck a needle in her arm. Lola blacked out.

A week later, Lola had calmed down. She had realized she had to stay in rehab facility court appointed after she reportedly attacked Sasha, in one of her drug induced binges. Vin had fled the country and left her unconscious on the floor. Janice had brought King back to America, which was paid by Sasha. But, since she hadn't been getting paid she was getting ready to leave King at a fire department, when Vita showed up at her door, stating to give her the baby.

King had been staying with her and it hurt Lola to now think of what she had become. After all these group meetings about feelings and life choices, Lola started to realize her choices were a one hundred percent reason for what had become of her life. She had become consumed with regret. She had to get better to get her son back. Lola knew Vita would never hurt her, but what if Uno had been keeping tabs on Vita like she said months ago.

She couldn't even fathom something happening to her baby. He was all she had left. She got out of bed going through her two pieces of luggage she had, looking for her jacket. As she dug through the suitcase she felt a stack of letters at the bottom. She pulled them out looking over the sender's name:

Inmate Rico Bailey #000555000D

Was the only thing she saw on the outside of the letter, her heart skipped a beat. She skimmed through all the letters reading his name on all the letters she looked at the dates on them all and decided to start with the oldest one.

So, many days she had wondered what happened to everyone. But, after that phone call from punk ass Quan she had assumed everyone turned their back on her. She opened the first letter.

Lo,

What's good, my nigga? I hope you doing a'ight. I've been thinking about you since the day I got in this motherfucker, but I'm good and we good. You were right about that nigga; I should've left him alone. But, lesson learned, ya' dig. I've got two and a half years. But, it's nothing. These niggaz can't keep a fly nigga like me down.

I guess you probably haven't heard that Cease died. Spoke to fam said didn't see you come thru the wake. Yea, it's fucked up. Damn, miss that nigga. But, I'm keeping this shit

*short for now. Just thought I would touch base with ya, and let
you know I'm always thinking about you.*

   Rico

   She sat up as tears began to form in her eyes. She
couldn't believe that Caesar was gone. Although, they
always got into spats he was her nigga one of her aces, she
thought all this time they had turned their back on her,
and that wasn't the case at all. As she read through a few
more letters he informed he'd gotten his G.E.D. and had
been reading a lot. Like most niggas he had begun reading
every hood novel, Mandela as well as the *Art of War*. He
had told Lola how he was planning to take what he
learned from it and applying it to his life.

   He had wrote about all the memories he and Lola
had shared, and all the laughs they had shared. They had
been friends since elementary school and he told her she
was one of the only people he genuinely trusted. He knew
that she would always have his back. Rico never asked for
her to put money on his books, just if she could send him
more magazines and books.

   She had been reading letters over two hours when
counselor walked in asking her was she going to dinner.
She said no and began another letter. In the fifth letter,
Rico told her he had not heard back from her yet and
assumed that she had not returned. He told her he wasn't
mad at her, that he always knew she would be the one to
get out of "Duval" first. At the end he asked her to send a
picture and more books if possible. She began to smile; she
could imagine his voice speaking to her. With his cocky
bravado, and pearly white smile always having something
slick to say. The fifth letter had a picture of her drawn

inside, which she thought was beautiful. She took a piece of tape, taping it to her wall. She stood up reading the sixth letter.

Lo,

What's good? I guess I see now why you haven't been answering my letters. I saw you on TV at the fucking Draft. Congratulations mama! Nigga can't lie, did a double look when your ass swayed across the screen. Who'd ever think you'd put the Timbs and wifebeaters away. (LOL) I said I know that's not my nigga Lo, sitting up there titties sitting nice and shit. You had me in here harder than a muthafucka! I can't front. But, you look good baby. So, you gonna be living on the west coast. That's what's up.

I guess I gotta say congratulations to you and that nigga, Dion. She laughed imagining him saying it sarcastically. *He better be good to you. I guess you got a good one… now when I get out of here I want some tickets. Ain't that just like a nigga. I'm just fucking with you. I'm happy for you. I'd be happier… if I heard from you. I can't help it you've been on my mind a lot. Ever since I saw you on television I can't get you out of my head. Fuck.*

She sat confused. The ending so abrupt. It was awkward, what exactly was he saying? Did he have feelings for her? She felt a knot building in her stomach almost like butterflies. She became lost in her thoughts when Carmen, her counselor came in and told her she had a phone call. She placed the letters under her pillow heading to the phones. It was Vita informing her she would bring King to visit her Saturday. She was happy to finally see her baby boy but all she could think about was kissing him and cradling him in her arms.

She then thought about Dion, and it always made her sad. She wondered if he would be happy for her and proud of the job she was doing with King. But, her mind would always wonder to the blur of time with Sasha and Vin. It made her cringe to think of how much she let herself go. Lola walked over to the closet where her luggage had been placed, opening her Louis Vuitton bag, where she had stashed bands of money from Sasha. She poured the contents over the bed, it was over four hundred thousand dollars, not bad she thought. *You still got it bitch. Me and King will be straight.* She then thought of Vita battling her demons. She had to get out of this rehab and get her baby.

She had been in rehab almost three months. She had read all of the letters from Rico and the letters gave her hope. They made her happy to know someone was thinking of her and wanting to be there for her. She had written him back weeks ago and gave him the number to reach her. Vita had been up every weekend with King he was getting bigger, and looked exactly like her. She decided she was going to move down to South Florida, since that city was the one place she had the happiest times in her life with Dion.

Vita schooled her to setting up a hair business. She had a distributor in which she had been getting hair from for years and she was going to set Lola up with their information so she could get settled. Vita had gotten with the realtor on Lola's California home and per Lola's permission, went into her savings and put down on a nice, South Florida home for Lola and King when she returned.

Vita was to come down to Miami with Lola to start up her business. But, Lola had another plan. She hadn't heard from Rico and she started to suspect the worse. She had checked on Nana and she informed her that no new letters had come. Lola had still been paying for nurse and meals on wheels. She was planning to bring her to Miami with her. Lola informed Anna soon as they were settled in they would move her down with them.

It was the day for her to leave and Vita was to meet her outside in a cab and Lola was to head straight to airport with King to Florida. When she arrived outside bag and tow, no Vita. She pulled out her phone preparing to dial Vita, her phone beeped displaying a text:

"Will meet you down in Florida with King. We missed flight will be on the next one available. Your car should be pulling up shortly. Welcome back bitch!"

She responded, "Thank you can't wait to see you two! Be safe with my luvie." Lola looked up seeing a Mercedes Sprinter pull along the curb. The driver got out opening the back door taking her bags. She glanced inside seeing bottles of Moet, Ciroc and bottles of water. She bypassed the alcohol, grabbing one of the bottles of water placing her bag on the seat. She grabbed a pair of shades from her purse placing over her eyes ready to head back home to the sunshine state to her new life.

Champagne Dreams & Legends

It had been two weeks since she left rehab. Vita came down last week with King and turned right around to board her flight back to Michigan. Lola was upset that they didn't spend any time together, or have time to catch up, nevertheless was happy to have her son back. He had grown so much, and although he was ecstatic to see her. She quickly noticed a change in her son. At times he seemed uncomfortable around her, the thought of King not knowing who she was crushed her. She reached back out to Janice who had moved to Texas. Janice agreed to come down, and Lola purchased a ticket for her to arrive the weekend.

Lola was impressed with the house Vita had purchased on her behalf. It was definitely out of the price budget she had set, but Vita assured her everything was paid in full, no worries. Nestled in a quiet, cul-de-sac in Coconut Creek, Florida it was the perfect location Lola wanted to restart her life, with a legal business. Two story, four bedroom, and three bath, she had well over enough space to be comfortable. She planned to drive up to Jacksonville to get nana, and bring her down as well. Her first plan of business was to start online business for the hair and check out a few boutique locations. She had got in touch with a realtor, and was to check out locations today. Lola arrived to the first location which was located inside a mall, which was not her prime location, but she decided to check it out anyway. Nancy Demoine, her realtor who was a middle aged, brunette, with vintage taste, had come highly recommended from Vita's contacts, she worked with a few a list celebrities and her pulling up in a Maybach with driver, made Lola do a second glance.

Lola stepped out walking over to the backseat to pick up King from his car seat. Dressed casually in a pair of high waist skinny jeans and a white slim fit tee, Louboutin's on her feet. Her hair pulled back in a sleek ponytail. She placed King in the stroller with a juice. Nancy strolled over to her. "Lola?"

"Please call me Lauren."

She replied with an extended arm.

"It's a pleasure to meet you. I know this is not your ideal location, however I thought you may have a second opinion once you view in person. I also hope you don't mind, I have invited another client who is looking to open a shoe store to view as well."

"No problem. Get your money honey. I'm certain this location may not have the vibe I'm looking for, but I will try to remain optimistic." Nancy nodded escorting her into the side entrance. Once entered into the hallway, they were greeted by security guards. The first glanced over Lola's derriere as she passed. At the last door, Nancy held it opened as Lola walked in. The location definitely had character all white treatments, and black shelves. Lola was impressed. There was a group of men leaning over the counter as one recorded himself by the shelves. He paused seeing Nancy and Lola enter. He smiled, giving a nod before walking over towards them. Lola looked over his outfit, he was wearing blue distressed jeans, white shirt and wheat Timberland boots. Ten necklaces hung from his neck. He shook Nancy's hand before locking eyes again with Lola. "I knew I remember your pretty ass from somewhere."

Lola side eyed his misplaced compliment, before taking in his face again. He definitely caught her eye, and had her attention with his full beard. "You remember me? Met you in Atlanta at a party." Lola's mind quickly tried to piece where she had met him. She immediately thought of Uno, and the *flawless* night. "Legend?"

He smiled happy she remembered. "Legend and Lola sound good together right." He replied confidently. Lola looked down at King who was resting on his side in stroller. "I guess I'm supposed to be gassed 'cause you remember who I am."

"It is a privilege to be in my presence. A, it was nice to see you again Legend would have been nice. Followed by how you been?" He folded his arms across his chest.

"Boy, bye. I only spoke with you for a few seconds, we do not know each other. I don't care anything about what you up to."

His friends laughed out loud. "She cold blooded, my nigga."

Legend glanced back over her body. "Nance... I'm taking the place. Don hit her with the bag. He placed his arm around Lola bringing her body in close to his. He leaned in to her ear. "See you at Prive Saturday, wear something sexy." He licked his lips, placing a stack of money in her hand. She rolled her eyes.

"I'm not going."

He smiled signaling his crew, to head towards the door. Don gave Nancy the bag of cash. Nancy looked over to Lola, Lola walked over to the counter she pulled out her ruby woo lipstick and wrote *"FUCK YOU"* on the counter. She smiled throwing the lipstick on the floor. "Make sure Prince Charming gets that message Nancy. We're done today." Lola strolled out with King in tow with no intentions of seeing Legend again.

Saturday afternoon, Janice had put King down for his nap and was folding his clothes as Lola looked online for decorative items for her boutique. The doorbell rang, startled Lola crept over to the window seeing a sprinter van parked along the curb. She walked over to her bedroom grabbed her .380 placing in the small of her back "Who is it?" She shouted.

"Have a delivery for a Lola?" The woman shouted from behind the door. She peeped thru the peephole, immediately thinking she needed better security around her home. There was flowers covering the entrance. Lola opened the door seeing vases of red roses everywhere. "What the fuck!" she replied as she looked around her foyer littered with roses. There was a total of four sprinters outside doors opened filled with roses. "Hi, Lola? May we bring these in for you?"

"Who are these from? Are you serious?"

She handed her a card. "Since you love red, I figured I'd return the favor and fill your home with something beautiful instead of a fuck you." Lola immediately laughed out loud. She escorted the drivers in with flowers one by one, her living room and foyer was filled with red. After all the flowers were inside the drivers came in with shopping bags. Givenchy, Gucci, Chanel, Sophia Webster and Balenciaga. "What the hell is going on here?" As the last bag was brought in Lola shook her head. *Was he crazy? How'd he get her address?* As the drivers piled back into their sprinters Lola closed the door looking over everything. She ran her fingers thru her hair debating what she was going to do with all this. Janice walked out of the bedroom. "Oh my goodness. Someone loves you."

"No. Someone is crazy."

Her doorbell rang again. She walked over looking thru the peep hole seeing a Givenchy Blue totem backpack. She opened the door seeing Legend standing in front of her a smile on his face. "So you wouldn't come to me tonight, so I figured I would come to you? He removed his shades, signaling to his security at the end of the driveway. You gonna let me in or leave me on the porch?" Lola invited him in. She closed the door behind them, she immediately pinned him to the door grabbing him by the chin. "What is your problem? You come over my house unannounced, sending flowers and shit! What the fuck?!"

"This face you make when you mad, is sexy as fuck. He smiled, as her body was pressed against his. He looked directly in her eyes removing her grip from his face, he gripped her face in the same way gently. My name is Kamal. A nigga can't do nothing nice for you. A thank you would be appreciated."

She swatted his hand away from her face. He pulled her in to him again. She reached for her gun in her waist. "Looking for this?" He waived the gun in her face.

Lola backed up. "What is up with you? I have my son in here?"

"I'm good, calm down. I'm not here to harm you or no shit like that. I came here to talk with you. He threw his hands up. You haven't been answering any of my calls, couldn't find you on social media. Made Nance give me your information for a couple dollars. He handed her back the gun. I've been thinking about you since Uno party. I saw you looking at me the entire night."

Lola thought back to the party she remembered glancing at him a few times, but immediately looking away for fear of Uno causing a scene. "Are you still signed with Uno?"

"Nah independent. So can we sit down and talk? I want to get to know you." Lola pulled her hair back out of her face, sliding the gun down in her purse in the kitchen. She walked towards the living room, inviting him to follow. He took off the back pack resting it on the table before sitting down on loveseat, beside Lola. She rolled her eyes sitting up making sure there was adequate space between them. "So do you make it a practice to stalk women and show up to their door?"

He chuckled. "Got jokes? Nah, like I said was trying to reach out to you. Couldn't find you. Only person I knew had a way to contact you was Nance so I said I'mma shoot my shot. Feel me?"

"Well, here we are. So what's up? To be honest I'm not looking to be in a relationship with anyone right now. Trying to spend as much time as I can with my son, to make up for lost time."

"I respect that. What's your son's name?

"King."

"Nice, like that. So what were you planning on doing with the location the other day?"

"Well, if you must know. I'm going into the hair business. I have high quality Malaysian bundles and I am opening a boutique."

"Selling hair? You too pretty to be doing that basic shit everybody else doing feel me. You gon do that, you gotta make your shit different from that same bullshit ads see on Instagram and Snapchat all day."

"So, now you are my marketing team? What the hell is Instagram?"

"You don't know what Instagram is? That's the first step of you fucking up, you gotta build shit on there, build you a following get endorsements and shit. I can help you with that, I'm the King of social media. Lola suddenly became interested in what he had to say. You need to go in your app store now and get all of these social media apps." Lola picked up her phone and downloaded the apps as he called them out to her. Once downloaded she began entering her email information and was time to enter a username, she stopped trying to think of a good username. He looked over on her phone.

"What up?"

"I can't think of a username."

"Let me see your phone" He typed in a user name and bio. He handed her back the phone. She read over the user name "*LoLegend*"

"Really? And it says I have one follower?" She clicked on the page and seen it was him. He had a blue check by his name Legend and over 50M followers and was only following one person, her. "You have fifty million followers what the fuck does that mean?"

He smiled. "Means I have more than one hustle and I'm gonna make sure niggas know who you are, so you'll be living beyond selling bullshit ass hair. Too sexy for that. Let me help you with your first post." He went inside his bag handing her a gift bag. The bag was slightly heavy the first box was Patek Philippe she looked into his eyes not believing he would have purchased her something that expensive. She removed the gift bow on top, opening the box revealing a flooded rose gold diamond & pearl Gondolo watch. It was beautiful. "Thank you… this is beautiful." He smiled.

"You're welcome. He took her arm placing the watch on her wrist. Lola couldn't help but smile at the two hundred and fifty one diamonds in dial. Don't thank me yet, there's more in there ain't it. She reached back into the bag, there was another box. A simple black box, she removed the bow as she did before. Opening the box revealed a set of keys. She picked them up confused. There was a small envelope below the keys, she opened it. In caps it read *"Fuck you too! You can have it!"*

"You can have that spot. I bought it for you along with the fuck you case."

Lola burst into laughter. "Are you crazy? You don't know me?" "I've been thinking about you since the first time I saw you. No strings. Have Nance and your people look over the paperwork." He looked into her eyes. Now let me help you with that post. He placed his wrist beside hers showing his diamond flooded Patek Philippe watch. She looked over the hundred dollar rose tattoo which sat on top of his hand.

He took her phone snapping a picture. Uploading to her account. The caption: #Legendaryshit.

"That's not all, I have a chef outside to prepare us some lunch."

"Are you serious?"

The doorbell rang and Lola walked over to answer the door. She looked thru the peephole seeing someone in a white jacket. A young woman emerged. "Hello, we have been sent on behalf of Mr. Legend to prepare you lunch. My name is Chelsea I will be your server, and this is Chef Boule." She shook both of their hands. Lola glanced back at Legend before opening the door and a team of servers walked in with trays in their hands. She stepped back from the door escorting everyone to her kitchen and dining room. Legend walked over to the dining room, he pulled out Lola's s chair, before sitting down. The server, Chelsea, a young brunette lit a candelabra on the table, bringing over an arrangement of fifty white and red roses.

"I figured we could chop it up. While we wait on the food." Chelsea poured champagne in their glasses before exiting back to the kitchen.

"So, I must ask. This lunch arrangement, this is not going to be an everyday thing. I'm not with that shit."

Legend chuckled. "Ain't no crazy fuck shit. Like what you had with that nigga. I've heard about that nigga and his meal bullshit. However, I wouldn't mind a few meals cooked by you every once in a while." He replied with a mischievous grin.

"Who says I can cook?" She replied defiantly.

"They have classes for that. We don't have to worry about that if I'm hungry, I know how to feed myself. And I don't need a chaperone every time I do so." Lola scoffed. Low key loving his responses, she admired how he didn't back down to her negative responses and always came back with a positive solution.

"I *know* how to cook." She replied dryly.

"I know." He raised his glass in the air motioning for Lola to lift her as well. "What are we toasting to?"

"To us. Building empires, success, blessings and always securing that bag. Ya dig."

She smiled, before their glasses touching. "I can toast to that." Legend smiled mumbling under his breath before sipping from his glass. Lola followed his lead sipping from her glass smelling the aroma of Jerk chicken filtered thru the room. It smelled amazing, her stomach began to growl anticipating the meal.

"So tell me about you Miss Lauren."

"Maybe... you should tell me about you."

"Nah, ladies first." He clasped his hands together, staring into her eyes. Chelsea entered with spring salads topped with fruit as they requested.

"What is it you want to know?"

"Whatever you want to tell me."

An hour later they had eaten their meal and were awaiting dessert. Lola was intrigued. Legend, birth name Kamal, was attractive, charismatic, and his swag was on ten. She felt herself more piqued by his backstory. She admired that he was humble, yet there was no bullshit to him. Kamal was born and raised in California with both parents. His parents had separated when he was five, and his mother kept the children.

His younger sister, Keilani, affectionately called Baby was his heart. She was sixteen and lived with his mother. Kamal informed her of his past crimes as a street fighter. Which is where he received his name for his one blow KO reputation. After numerous fights and an undisputed record, he soon received death threats, and suffered a few injures which were nothing to him compared to his repercussions to his assailants. Each injury was a result of a sneak, and his retaliation resulted in a brutal bruise to their physical and ego.

He began writing rhymes and battle rapping while in juvie. He took his time studying the game as he did with fighting, buying every album from: *Tupac Shakur, Too Short, Nas, The Wutang Clan, Scarface, TI, Snoop Dogg and Jay-Z*. A friend posted a video of one of his battles on social media and the video shortly went viral. Soon leading to top producers and execs in his DM's offering deals and flights to their offices all over the country. That had been two years ago. He had capitalized on the exposure and began posting weekly studio sessions, recording his journey to the music industry which soon made him a household name. He had Lola's complete attention. His piercing eyes which had a fire behind them was attractive to her. His build muscular and powerful, a solid possible one eighty, she could see herself being smothered in his hold. He made a point to explain he used no drugs, and drank only on occasions socially. He was strictly about building his brand, and making sure he could dabble in as many lanes as possible to keep every avenue open and not limit himself to just the music industry. Damn, got to love a man with ambition.

A New Normal

Three months later Lola and Kamal, had been spending almost every day together. From the initial post her followers quickly went from one to twenty thousand, and was currently at one million and counting. After the first few posts of her shopping and playing with King went viral, she and Legend had become *bae watch* topics on *The Shade Room*. Designers and makeup companies began to send her free merchandise, leaving her garage overflowing. Kamal had been a breath of fresh air. He reminded her of her past in Duval, he kept her laughing in tears and had become close with King. Lola adored his relationship with King.

Legend was currently in New York City promoting his new single, which had immediately shot to number one. Lola was at home preparing her car this weekend was to be the day she was to move Anna to Miami with her. She was ecstatic, Lola purchased her a Tempur-Pedic bed for Anna's master room with private bathroom, walk in closet and recliner with fifty inch television. Lola planned to surprise her and finally introduce her to King as well. Her phone rang interrupting her thoughts. She looked down at the screen seeing her assistant, Jazmin's name, she answered placing the phone on speaker.

"Hey Lo, I was calling to remind you about your plans tonight."

"Plans tonight?"

"Yes, you are to attend a boutique opening in S. Beach at five, you were to do press at the event, then you have an appearance at the club, a quick interview with

Jamz tonight in the mix and when Legend's flight comes in tonight, you two have an appearance at Diamonds to promote his single and reservations for dinner at one twelve?"

"What the hell? All of this today?"

"I've updated your calendar two days ago."

"I was planning to drive to Jacksonville today!"

"You would not have time for that and glam today. You also have press scheduled at each event."

"Damn! Okay, I want her here this week. You find someone to get her and I'll pay whatever."

"Okay, Lola I will make it happen." Lola hung up the phone in her feelings about her now cancelled plans of the day. She looked over to King who was seated in his high chair eating chopped French toast and sausage with Janice. Lola smiled at him. "Hi stanka! Give mama suga!" He smiled brightly showing his pegs, Lola kissed his lips, He grabbed her face. Janice grabbed the spare phone, snapping a picture of their exchange. Janice handed the phone to Lola to look over she smiled, posting the picture to her page with the heart emoji, #myeverything. By the time she placed the phone back on the table, her notifications began to go off repeatedly. She glanced over a few of the comments, one stood out.

Legend: King Shit! Crown emoji. Is that my sausage tho? Laughing face emoji.

Lola laughed out loud at his comment. Kamal as she affectionately called him, definitely had her smitten since the moment he stepped into her home. His sarcasm and humor matched hers, they both enjoyed being homebodies when need be, equal temperament although they had not argued once since the initial meeting. His assertiveness, let her know he wasn't to be played with. That spark in him she grew to admire, he stayed on his grind and made her a priority in everything he did. If he was in town he made sure his plans included her as his first stop. He had not moved in yet, but didn't want to. He had told her they needed to find a home together, to build their future in. As a man he couldn't invade on her space.

Lola was cool with his request, she realized they would need more space any way once Nana moved down. It would be a full house, she relished at the thought of having everyone under one roof. A huge family, something she always dreamed of. She walked over to the bathroom to wash her hands. Her phone began to ring alerting her she was receiving a Facetime call. She glanced over her reflection in the mirror pulling her tresses out her face, before accepting the call. "Hi Babe." She replied with a smile and squeaky voice which shocked herself.

"What up Baby! Lookin' good, turn around, let me see all of you." She blushed turning panning the phone over her body. She was dressed in a pair of Adidas floral leggings and crop top, her attire for road trip today, which she was still salty had been cancelled. As she panned over her derriere, he got closer to the camera. "Look at all of dat. She laughed, bringing the phone back up to her face. But this right here is most important seeing you with a smile, make up free." She had forgot that she only had moisturizer on her face, not even a hint of gloss on her lips. She now looked at the blemishes on her face.

"You beautiful! He replied in a joking matter mimicking a blogger that they enjoyed watching on social media. She smiled instantly. Just got my schedule, so me and you dinner. Then the club, we gon be in there for maybe two hours. You good with that? I know how you feel about club scene."

"Yeah, I'm fine with that. I'm about to have glam get me together I didn't realize I had a few appearances today. I am going to meet you at airport right?"

"Of course. Want to see you soon as I touch down. Manager said magazine wants to do a spread on us. I'll have him send you over details. Photo shoot will be in New York. I'm good with it if you are, if not it's a wrap with them."

"Sounds cool. Um, we can talk about it over dinner."

"Bet. So how my hitta? Besides eating up my food?"

"He is fine. In there with Janice being greedy." She walked out to the living room siting down.

"I copped King a few things while I was out here. Fly shit."

"Aww... thank you. That was very sweet of you! We appreciate it. You are going to have him spoiled!" Her doorbell rang and she heard Jazmin on her phone and several footsteps followed, she knew it was her glam team with today and tonight's looks. "Lola... are you ready?" said Jazmin from the kitchen.

"Yea... she replied. She looked back down at the screen. Well, that's Jaz, gotta get beat for these appearances honey."

"A'ight. It's all good. See you tonight."

Lola looked at the screen blowing air kisses to him. "Later Babe."

"Later baby."

She went into the den area which had been turned into her own glam area, located in the back of house. She looked down at the phone making sure Legend was disconnected. A reminder came up on her screen. *"Meet Vita in Orlando."* It had slipped her mind Vita was to be in Orlando, that weekend and on her way to Jacksonville she was to meet up with her. *I gotta call her.* She thought.

"Heyy gorgeous. I pulled some sexy looks for you today. I would like you to go over a few to see which stands out to you." Lola looked over the two racks of clothes which were brought in. Balmain, Givenchy, Versace were a few that popped out to her as she ran her fingers across a few of the pieces. She immediately stopped on a Sophia Webster bodysuit. "I'm feeling this first. For tonight I want something short and sexy for babe. He loves to see my legs." Her stylist smiled. "I have two more racks for you." She went outside, with the makeup artist pulling in two more racks, the items were red and nude colored. She smiled. The makeup artist came in with three bouquet of roses. "These last racks were handpicked for you by Legend."

"Of course they are. Lola stood up looking over the designer threads. Everything was short. Lola eyes fell on one nude piece. "Definitely this one for dinner." Everyone smiled at her selection. Jazmin walked over handing Lola a gift bag. There was a card on top of the small box inside. She opened the card.

It said *"This would look right with that fit."*

She opened the box it was a pear shaped four carat rose gold sapphire ring, with loose diamonds surrounding. She took the ring out of the box sliding it on her right middle finger, the huge stone which sat in center was everything. Jazmin looked over the ring. "It is amazing Lo."

"Is he Crazy?! I love it though." She pulled out her phone sending Legend a text. "The ring is fuckin amazing. I luv it!! xoxo" She opened Snapchat app, preparing to snap a picture, flipping the bird as she smiled seductively she captioned the video with heart emoji's. Jazmin's phone began to buzz with press calls. She ignored. "What would you like to say to press about the ring?"

Lola's makeup artist began to contour her face, Lola's phone beeped with a message.

"You're more than welcome, sexy, Just a day in the life, when you fuck with a legendary nigga."

She smiled mischievously as she responded back. "You just bring that legendary D tonight."

#Goals

After leaving first event, Lola was whisked away in a Range Rover to meet Legend at airport. She glanced over her phone, seeing King walking down the hall as the lock screen. The ring had her mood on ten all day. When asked about the ring at first event she had said it was a gift and she dodged the engaged questions. Lola unlocked her phone sending a quick text to Janice to for an update. Janice sent her a video of King in the tub. She responded to the video with smiling face emoji and thank you.

"I have uploaded all of your images from tonight with fans to your IG. Legend's flight should be in, in twenty minutes."

"Okay. She opened her snapchat app, filming herself with a flower wreath filter. *What up everyone! Thank you to everyone who came out and showed love at the Love Bar grand opening tonight. Had an amazing time, I hope to see all of you tonight at Diamonds!*" She blew a kiss to camera at the end of video, before snapping a picture of her thigh high crystal Giuseppe sandals, and her ring. Captioned *"When going to see bae…"*

At the airport terminal paparazzi were outside waiting on her arrival. One part of her new normal she hated was the paps constant harassment. Jazmin stepped out first barricading Lola as she escorted her over to Maybach which was waiting. They immediately swarmed her snapping pictures, she slid a pair of Dolce & Gabbana shades over her eyes.

Lola!! Lola!! Are you and Legend engaged? How do you feel about his nominations? Who are you wearing you look amazing?

The driver opened the backdoor, Lola slid into the seat tossing her curls over her shoulder. Their voices became elevated as Legend emerged out of the terminal doors. Dressed in a Gucci shirt, jeans and Jordan sneakers on his feet.

Legend! Legend! What can we expect on the album? How many features? Are you going to marry Lola? How do you feel about you two being labeled goals? The driver opened the door the paps swarmed in with pictures again as his security warded them off.

"Of course one day I'm gonna lock that down. One day. Have you seen my baby?" Lola smiled hearing his response he had told her that before, when they were alone. But to hear him speak it to the world sent butterflies in her stomach. He slid into the backseat. "What up baby! Come here!" Lola opened her snapchat app ready to capture the moment. He pulled her into his arms, kissing her neck and lips passionately. His scent his favorite Life Savers wint o green mints mixed with Dior cologne. She brushed her wild curls out of her face mounting him. He looked into her eyes, palming her ass. She continued recording as she licked the side of his face and lips, captioning the snap "Hey Daddy..." She tossed the phone on her seat.

"How was your flight babe?"

"It was a'ight. Always gotta get that bag. He caressed her face. Missed you mooshu."

"Told you about calling me that!" She replied with a smile.

"It's all love. No shade. You know you my chyna doll. He looked over her dress caressing her curves. I knew this was gonna look right on you, moment I saw this shit." He looked over the nude, crystal studded dress she was wearing. She began to grind her body slowly against him, soon his hands were under her dress. Lola smiled as he pulled her thong to the side running his finger over her clit. Her lips parted, she leaned forward kissing his ear gently as she tugged on his ear with her teeth. "Yo, we need to stop by the room... FontaineBleau before dinner."

"I'm gonna need Jazmin to bring me a new dress huh?"

"You already know..." She laughed out loud, as he removed his fingers licking them.

"At least get a few pictures of me in it." She kissed his lips gently. We can handle that."

An hour later, the glam team had arrived to their Sorrento penthouse suite. Lola sat in the chair with her now limp curls dressed in one of Legend's promotional tees and nude lace panties. Her crystal sandals were now skewed across the floor. Her stylist was going over new choices for tonight. Legend had showered and was in a Givenchy plaid cross inset button down, Saint Laurent distressed jeans, and Timberland boots on his feet. His stylist placed his three diamond chains on his neck. He walked over to Lola, to see if she had made her decision. She looked over his outfit. "You look handsome babe. Come here." He walked over to her, resting his body in between her legs. She kissed him slowly, caressing his face as she tugged at his beard.

"Don't start nothin' you can't finish." Legend replied with a smile. She laughed out loud. "I would, but we have places to be." She wrapped her legs around his body, her makeup artist started to highlight her face. She released her grip from his body sitting back up straight so that she could finish her makeup. "You nasty." Replied Legend with a smile. He pulled out his phone recording himself.

We on our way. Someone trying to be nasty and make us late. He panned over to Lola. "Whateva! You are the reason we are still here… couldn't keep your hands to yourself! She licked her lips sensually. He placed the camera back on himself. *A'ight, that's enough of my mooshu showing y'all niggas her tongue and shit.* Lola laughed. "Kamal… go. She will never finish my makeup with you in here with me." He placed his hands up in the air in defeat walking towards the bedroom.

Everyone laughed, their chemistry always brought a certain energy in the room. They were in love, there was no point in hiding it, and they couldn't if they tried. Her stylist held two dresses in the air. "I like the black." Said Lola. Legend looked back. "Definitely the black."

"Black. I have a black pair of the same shoes I had on earlier right?"

"Yes. I'll get them. That was simple. For once."

"How rude. I'm a great client."

"Oh please, King is a better client. So sweet and go with the flow."

"I guess I can't argue with that. King is the best."

The ambience outside the restaurant had been chaotic. Paparazzi everywhere, they were seated in a secluded area in the back where the curtains had been closed. The server, a Latina mid-thirties named Naomi, brought a bottle of champagne over filling their glasses. They were enjoying their spring salad with strawberries and cashews. Lola looked across the table at Kamal, staring into his chestnut eyes. He was looking down at his food, he looked over to her.

"A busy week ahead. New Orleans, Houston, Detroit, and Chicago next week. Radio shit. Back to New York, and Cali. I would like you and King to come out with me to NYC, and Cali. I want to show you around my city."

"We can do that. Have to make sure my calendar is free, but I will need to make sure Janice will be available as well."

"No problem. I'll make sure Janice set. Have my team handle all reservations."

"Okay. Sounds like a plan." Her mind immediately went back to Cali and memories of Dion. For the first time she did not feel the pain which she normally felt when he came to mind. Her mind immediately went to an image of Kamal and happy times. *Was she in love?* Her thoughts were interrupted by the sound of his voice

"Damn, how did they get that shot tho?!"

"What?" He handed her his phone. It was a blog site, the picture was of her mounted on his lap, her hand with sapphire rock on his face. The headliner said, *Legend & Lo, bae goals, engaged?"* She laughed.

"Really we're engaged? Why do they want us married so bad? She handed him back the phone.

"I don't know. But when I do, it won't be a rock like that. I want that shit to sit up like this."

He picked up a piece of strawberry placing on top of his finger. "This shit not even big enough. The strawberry fell into his plate. Anyway, why would we share everything else and hide that?"

"Right. I can hear Vita cussing me out right now. Speaking of which let me message her." Legend smiled at her. Vita was not someone he was fond of but he didn't want to come between her and her girl.

"What can she say to you? Heard she got some shit in her closet herself?"

"What do you mean?"

"It's just something about her, man. I remember when I was handling meetings with Uno she was around. She bugged out."

"You said she has shit in her closet? What did you mean by that?"

"Ask her about her skeletons, shit. Everyone at the label used to have all types of shit on her. Call that bitch crazy. I told you, you should stop hanging wit' her."

"You fuck her?" Lola replied cringing inside praying he wouldn't say yes.

"Hell nah. She not my type. I've already told you need to cut all ties with that broad." Lola looked into his eyes again.

"Well… everyone has skeletons in their closet. I know mines isn't caviar and roses. Would you cut me off over my past?"

"You taking this personal. I'm only telling you to watch yourself around that broad, mooshu."

"I mean I do feel some sort of way. Vi is my sister, my ace… Yes she may have a dark past but so do I. I wasn't always this sexy bitch. I had to do what I had to do to feed my family as well."

"Come here. I didn't mean to offend you. He walked over to her side of the table. He kissed her cheek. You good?"

"Yes we're good."

"Give me a kiss." She kissed his lips. He walked back over to his seat. Lola's mind began to wander, *what did he mean?* Vita was her best friend, had been there through her darkest times. Yes, she was crazy and popped pills. Vita was her sister, the realest bitch she had ever met. She sipped her Moet, rolling her eyes to the thought of cutting off her bestie.

Glass Houses

Two days later, Lola was at the gym working out with her trainer. She decided to work out every day before the photo shoot. Jazmin had received treatments for shoot and they wanted her in a bikini and chinchilla coat. As she did lounges with weights around her ankles and five pound dumbbells in each hand. "Three more Lauren! You got this!" shouted her trainer Adrianne. She continued across the floor to the other side. Once to the other side, her phone rang. The trainer brought it over to her. She looked over to the phone seeing Janice on the screen, she dropped the dumbbells answering the phone.

"Hello." She replied short of breath.

"Lauren! Lauren! Janice never called her Lauren, her defenses immediately went up."

"Janice, what's up? What's goin' on?"

"Man, have been coming to house. I see on cameras with mask. I'm scared should I call police?"

"What?! Where are you? What did he look like? I'm on my way!!" Lola snatched the gloves off her hands. "I have to go." She grabbed her keys from the counter, snatching the weights from her ankles. She rushed out to the parking garage, overcome with emotion. Once inside of her car, she sat behind the wheel. Her chest heaved up and down, she pursed her lips trying to take slow breaths. Frustration welled up inside of her as she punched the steering wheel. She reached across the seat opening the glove box to retrieve her gun. An arm clasped around her neck choking her, before covering her mouth with a cloth soaked in substance.

*   *   *

The room was dark and cold. All that could be heard was the swinging of a chain and the scent of cigars and alcohol. Lola looked around realizing she was on the floor of some sort of warehouse. She looked down realizing she had handcuffs around her wrists and her ankles was shackled to a long chain. Naked and nipples erect she crawled around the floor, before running into a wall. She sat up against it, the cool of the wall sent a chill up her spine. A lamp flickered on in the room footsteps followed clicking as it neared closer. Lola squinted her eyes, ready to see her assailant.

"Yuh, don't get it do yuh? It's never over for me and yuh, mi pretty." Hearing his voice sent a rage inside of her, she immediately closed her legs.

"Fuck you! You sick muthafucka! Where am I?"

"Yuh don't get to ask me shit! He picked up a glass which was on the table, tossing it at her head. It shattered as it hit the wall above her, the pieces falling into her face. She shielded her eyes, before placing her hands to her side. Uno appeared in front of her dressed in all red, as if the devil himself. "I advise you to do everything I say!"

"Fuck you!" She spat at him.

"Oh… here is the *real* Lauren, or is this stick up bitch Lola. Lola cut her eyes at him. Yea… let mi tell yuh a little story. I met with an investor said he had a deal on exclusive imported cars. He said that his fam drove transport trucks and was looking for a steady job. I said good I need another means of transporting my product from Miami. Lola's eyes widened. Figured it was a win-win situation, could get deals on mi cars and product on one shipment. Driver calls me in Jacksonville and said that he was in transit with my Maserati, Ferrari, Lamborghini and Tesla among others. I receive a call mi driver dead. Majority of mi cars are damaged and totaled. More importantly, none of mi product was recovered. To mi surprise, nigga who I practically raised and put on to game is the one behind the hit. I know yuh pretty little head thinking who could that be? We'll get to that later, have plenty of time for that. Well, I do... not yuh. You're soaked in alcohol, beautiful. Then this pretty china doll comes into mi city at mi party. Mi team said she pulled up in a Ferrari, minute I saw her I had to have her. Fucked up and fell hard for her. I was willing to let yuh go, to Mr. Nice guy, ball player. Yuh know after yuh torched mi place, I was willing to let yuh have a clean slate and marry that punk. But, she couldn't... she had fallen in love with yuh. Hated how much everyone loved yuh. Yuh had happiness and a child... something my *wife* could never have."

Lola looked to him letting the words register in her head. *This nigga say wife? The fuck?* It suddenly became clear.

"Yuh thought I was your only enemy and here she was under yuh the whole time, taking everything from yuh. I didn't pop your little ball player, she did. Couldn't stand to see yuh happy. Yuh allowed her in with open arms. Rage boiled inside of her as she took in everything he was saying to her. When she thought of Dion a tear streamed down her cheek. I controlled every move yuh made. When yuh became a dancer, dollhouse is my club, yuh worked for me. The houses yuh lived in… I own, including your current home. Vin, is my business partner. He did everything I told him to. Every time you fucked him, I arranged it… The way I see it yuh were fuckin' me. Sasha tour, I put yuh there. I own yuh! You've been my property, mi investment. When I looked into who stole mi shipment, and seen a bullshit Duval crew, who had been hittin' niggas up for years took my shit, I needed answers. I received information finding out mi patna, Rico Bailey was in Raiford… and only had one visitor on his books… guess who that was… Lauren fuckin Rose. The same bitch who slept in mi bed, same bitch I fucked daily." His voice rose with aggression.

"As I see it, yuh owe me. Four hundred million dollars. For my cars and product yuh and your pussy ass crew stole from me. I want mi fuckin' money and Rico! I know he is out of prison and has been on the low. Yuh are gonna pay me with your life, and your son's life or your sweet nana's life. I paid your sweet nana a visit, sad she may be a casualty of your bullshit."

Lola bit her lip, nervously wishing she had her gun to shoot him between his eyes right now. "Oh, miss Lola pissed now huh? Where your *Legendary* nigga now? Parading that fuck nigga on social media. Everywhere I turn pictures and videos of yuh with that bitch plastered in every blog. I made my own story and sent it to *Mr. Legendary*. He pressed play on the video, displaying him raping her on the same warehouse floor. Couldn't let that good pum pum go to waste, had to taste one last time. Still like I remember it. He licked his fingers. Slightly off… yuh pregnant? Too bad today will be yuh last."

Lola rolled her eyes refusing to give him any interaction. "Come on use those pretty lips. I know what will make yuh speak. Come! He shouted."

In walked Vita in a long white maxi dress with King in her arms, black and ruby ring on her finger. A grin plastered on her face. "He's such a sweetie pie. He should've been mine! He deserves a mother who can spend time with him and love him instead of parading her ass on social media. So naïve."

"Give mi the baby." Said Uno. She handed him King. King looked over to Lola seeing her on the floor. "Mama… mama." Screamed King looking at her on the floor.

"Hi… Luvie." She replied with a smile in an attempt to calm him.

Vita walked over to Lola. Lola's eyes piercing as she looked over the woman who was once her ace, sister and confidant. She had betrayed her like no other. Vita squatted down in front of her. "Why do you deserve everything? A dusty, raggedy, pill popping bitch like you. Why do you deserve a beautiful baby, and happily ever after bullshit! You're not better than me! Everything you have I created. I put you on, bum bitch! I allowed you to fuck my husband! I allowed you into *my* world and you thought you were better than me. We are going to take everything from you! Starting with your worthless ass life."

Lola stared into her eyes. "I guess bitches who live in glass houses shouldn't throw stones eh?" as the last word left her lips she grabbed Vita with her cuffed hands jamming the broken glass into her neck. She cuffed her in between her legs. She began stabbing her in the eyes repeatedly with glass as she shrieked in horror, blindly swatting her hands to pry Lola off. "You shiesty ass lying muthafucka. You will never open your fuckin' eyes again! This is for D! Fuck you!" Uno shouted for back up before handing off the baby to one of his men. The attack happened so fast he was stunned. He rushed over to them kicking Lola in the face, she fell back unto the wall. Vita began to gurgle on her own blood, he motioned for his men to get Vita out immediately. Rage in his eyes he stepped on Lola's hand which held the glass. She screamed out in pain as the glass pierced through her own palm. Vita began to convulse Uno looked over to her. "Get her to a fuckin doctor now! Go!! Have the men outside in position." They ushered her out of the warehouse and into waiting vehicles.

"Yuh try to kill my wife eh?"

"Fuck you and that crazy bitch. If you are gonna end me do it now, muthafucka! 'Cause I'm gonna kill you and that bitch if she's not dead already."

"Is that a threat?" He replied with a smile.

"A fuckin' promise, you weak dick, pussy ass muthafucka." She replied as the blood leaked from her mouth. Uno fired a shot hitting her in her shoulder she screamed out in pain. He walked towards her.

"What yuh call me bitch?"

"You heard what the fuck she said! Pussy ass nigga! Uno turned around. Yea, get a good look at my face muthafucka. You wish you could look this fresh!" entered a male voice. Uno fired his gun missing as he returned fire one shot to Uno's chest. Lola looked over trying to see who it was. Uno doubled over in pain unto his stomach. "Heard you was looking for me. Well here I am muthafucka." He walked over firing another shot to the back of Uno's head. Uno's body crashed to the floor. Lola looked up with a smile on her face.

"What up, Lo money?"

"My nigga…." She looked into his eyes he had put on a few pounds which looked good on him. His cut low and clean as it had always been. He reached down with the key he had lifted off one of Uno's security men and unshackled her feet. He looked in her eyes as he unlocked the cuffs on her wrists. As the second cuff dropped from her wrists, she attempted to place her arms around his neck to hug him.

"Rico…"

"Shh… he looked into her eyes, he grabbed her chin kissing her lips. His lips soft and warm, his scent etched in her memory, sent a warm feeling thru her body. I got you, Lo." He took his shirt off his back placing it over her head and body. Let's go get that shit closed."

He placed her in his arms carrying her out towards the entrance. She looked back at Uno stretched out on the floor. As they walked out of the room, the front door of the warehouse opened. In walked Legend dressed in all black, glock in hand, with a group of goons behind him. "Lola!" He walked over to Rico, grabbing her out of his arms. Rico grimaced, looking over her body. He hugged her body tightly, kissing her face. "Owww… "

"Sorry… baby. You okay?"

"I was shot in the shoulder. Where is my baby and nana?" She stood in front of them both.

"I saw King outside in a car he's good."

"Where's nana playboy?" said Rico.

"Who the fuck is this?" said Legend defensively.

"Her nigga."

"What? Lauren what up? Who this?"

"Choose." Said Rico.

Lola held her shoulder in pain. She looked over at both men. One was the love of her life, the other had her heart. Emotions filled her heart as she thought of the decision she had to make. She looked back and forth into their eyes. She sighed walking over to him. "I love you. I appreciate everything you have ever done for me. But, the life we created is not where I want to be anymore. I'm not the person you know anymore." She kissed his cheek slowly and gently before taking the other man's hand walking out the door.

"I love you. Let's get you to a hospital."

"I love you too. How did you know where I was or what was going on? There's a lot that has happened with me I need to tell you?"

"I know. I've been following you since the day we met."

He held open the door allowing her to get in first. She looked back seeing King in the backseat as well as her nana. She burst into tears seeing their faces. She reached into the backseat hugging her nana. "Oh my god Nana! Are you okay?"

"I'm fine, my Lola. I knew God would eventually bring you to back to me." said Nana as she kissed the side of Lola's face. A driver sat behind the wheel. The door closed, Lola looked over to the warehouse seeing Legend's goon's outside the warehouse their faces sullen.

The car drove off down 95, the city lights illuminated in the Duval skyline. She breathed deeply taking in the city, which had been home to every first experience in her life. The city where she met her crew, and had met the man who had captured her heart. She smiled at the way he had come to her rescue. She looked up into her love's eyes he smiled back at her as he held her in his arms, kissing the top of her head softly as he cradled her body. A phone began to ring repeatedly. He reached in his pocket, pulling out the phone to answer it. "Clear everything for two weeks. I have to make sure my wife is okay." She looked into his eyes, kissing him on the lips. Happy with the decision she had made, but she knew from the first time he made her laugh, he was the one. She would never go back to what she was, too much had happened to ever go back. She relished at the fact of starting a new life and future with the man she had begun to build a *legendary* empire with.

"Welcome to my city babe."

He smiled at her. "Soon as we get that hole closed up you can show me around your city and tell me everything you want to tell me mooshu." She held her shoulder in pain.

"Let's get her to the nearest hospital, Easton. Now!"

"Baptist it is."

*   *   *

"Female... Patient. We may not be able to save the right eye. Deep laceration on neck and chest. Let's get oxygen and get her on the table immediately! The nurse placed her fingers on her wrist to retrieve a pulse. The nurses moved swiftly thru the room placing an IV to her arm. Let's do all that we can to save this woman."

"We're losing her..."

<u>More Books from Tanisha Renee</u>

Death Before Dishonor

Death Before Dishonor II: Secrets

Connect with author on Twitter: @realauthorista1

Instagram: @authorista

Hashtag with #teamlola #teamlegend #teamvita #teamuno

Death Before Dishonor III: Heavy is the Head. Coming Summer 2019!! #teamcash #teamsydney #teampreme #teamyogi